Her hair was loose now, all the pins discarded—presumably, Diana thought absently, on the carpets surrounding the divan, but the thought was vague. Irrelevant in comparison with that oh-so-sinuous languor stealing over her.

Nikos's fingers were still threading in her hair, softly smoothing her locks, just above her nape. Instinctively, she dipped her head farther, giving a little sigh of pleasure. She heard his low laugh again, felt his sensuously working fingertips move to the tops of her ears, then her pulse quickening as his thumb idly teased at the lobe. A million quivers of sensation went through her. It felt so good—

There was a haze around her. She felt her eyelids dip, made a little sound in her throat.

Felt, as she did, Nikos's hand stroke down her throat, its slender column caressed by his long, sensitive fingers. She felt her face turned toward him, felt her eyelids fluttering open—open to see him looking down at her.

And in his eyes, in the dim starlight, was what she could not deny.

Did not want to de

Julia James lives in England and adores the peaceful verdant countryside and the wild shores of Cornwall. She also loves the Mediterranean—so rich in myth and history, with its sunbaked landscapes and olive groves, ancient ruins and azure seas. "The perfect setting for romance!" she says. "Rivaled only by the lush tropical heat of the Caribbean—palms swaying by a silver-sand beach lapped by turquoise waters...what more could lovers want?"

Books by Julia James

Harlequin Presents

Securing the Greek's Legacy
The Forbidden Touch of Sanguardo
Captivated by the Greek
A Tycoon to Be Reckoned With
A Cinderella for the Greek

Secret Heirs of Billionaires

The Greek's Secret Son

Mistress to Wife

Claiming His Scandalous Love-Child
Carrying His Scandalous Heir

Visit the Author Profile page
at Harlequin.com for more titles.

Julia James

TYCOON'S RING OF CONVENIENCE

HARLEQUIN PRESENTS®

ISBN-13: 978-1-335-41961-3

Tycoon's Ring of Convenience

First North American publication 2018

Printed in U.S.A.

www.Harlequin.com

TYCOON'S RING OF CONVENIENCE

For JW and CE—with thanks.

CHAPTER ONE

THE WOMAN IN the looking glass was beautiful. Fair hair, drawn back into an elegant chignon from a fine-boned face, luminous grey eyes enhanced with expensive cosmetics, lips outlined with subtle colour. At the lobes of her ears and around her throat pearls shimmered.

For several long moments she continued to stare, unblinking. Then abruptly she got to her feet and turned, the long skirts of her evening gown swishing as she headed to the bedroom door. She could delay no longer. Nikos did not care to be kept waiting.

Into her head, in the bleak reality of her life now, came the words of a saying that was constantly there.

"'Take what you want," says God. "Take it and pay for it."'

She swallowed as she headed downstairs to her waiting husband. Well, she had taken what she'd wanted. And she was paying for it. Oh, how she was paying for it…

Six months previously

'You do realise, Diana, that with probate now completed and your financial situation clearly impossible, you have no option but to sell.'

Diana felt her hands clench in her lap, but did not reply.

The St Clair family lawyer went on. 'It won't reach top price, obviously, because of its poor condition, but you should clear enough to enable you to live pretty decently. I'll contact the agents and set the wheels in motion.'

Gerald Langley smiled in a way that she supposed he thought encouraging.

'I suggest that you take a holiday. I know it's been a very difficult time for you. Your father's accident, his progressive decline after his injuries—and then his death—'

He might have saved his breath. A stony expression had tautened Diana's face. 'I'm not selling.'

Gerald frowned at the obduracy in her voice. 'Diana, you must face facts,' he retorted, his impatience audible. 'You may have sufficient income from shares and other investments to cope with the normal running and maintenance costs of Greymont, or even to find the capital for the repairs your father thought were necessary, but this latest structural survey you commissioned after he died shows that the repairs urgently needed—that *cannot* be deferred or delayed—are *far* more extensive than anyone realised. You simply do not have the funds for it—not after death duties. Let alone for the decorative work on the interior. Nor are there any art masterpieces you can sell—your grandfather disposed of most of them to pay his own death duties, and your father sold everything else to pay *his*.'

He drew a breath,

'So, outside of an extremely unlikely lottery win,' he said, and there was a trace of condescension now, 'your only other option would be to find some extremely rich man with exceptionally deep pockets and marry him.'

He let his bland gaze rest on her for a second, then resumed his original thread.

'As I say, I will get in touch with the agents, and—'

His expression changed to one of surprise. His client was getting to her feet.

'Please don't trouble yourself, Gerald.' Diana's voice was as clipped as his. She picked up her handbag and made her way to the office door.

Behind her she heard Gerald standing up. 'Diana—what are you doing? There is a great deal more to discuss.'

She paused, turning with her hand on the door handle. Her gaze on him was unblinking. But behind her expressionless face emotions were scything through her. She would *never* consent to losing her beloved home. Never! It meant everything to her. To sell it would be a betrayal of her centuries-old ancestry and a betrayal of her father, of the sacrifice he'd made for her.

Greymont, she knew with another stabbing emotion, had provided the vital security and stability she'd needed so much as a child, coping with the trauma of her mother's desertion of her father, of herself... Whatever it might take to keep Greymont, she would do it.

Whatever it took.

There was no trace of those vehement emotions as she spoke. 'There is nothing more to discuss, Gerald. And as for what I am going to do—isn't it obvious?'

She paused minutely, then said it.

'I'm going to find an extremely rich man to marry.'

Nikos Tramontes stood on the balcony of his bedroom in his luxurious villa on the Cote d'Azur, flexing his broad shoulders, looking down at Nadya, who was swimming languorously in the pool below.

Once he had enjoyed watching her—for Nadya Serensky was one of the most outstandingly beautiful of the current batch of celebrity supermodels, and Nikos had enjoyed being the man with exclusive access to her. It had sent a clear signal to the world that he had arrived—had acquired the huge wealth that a woman like Nadya required in her favoured men.

But now, two years on, her charms were wearing thin, and no amount of her pointing out what a fantastic couple they made—she with her trademark flaming red hair, him with his six-foot frame to match hers, and the darkly saturnine looks that drew as many female eyes as her spectacular looks drew male eyes—could make them less stale. Worse, she was now hinting—blatantly and persistently—that they should marry.

Even if he had not been growing tired of her, there would be no point marrying Nadya—it would bring him nothing that he did not already have with her.

Now he wanted more than her flame-haired beauty, her celebrity status. He wanted to move on in his life, yet again. Achieve his next goal.

Nadya had been a trophy mistress, celebrating his arrival in the plutocracy of the world—but now what he wanted was a trophy *wife*. A wife who would complete what he had sought all his life.

His expression darkened, as it always did when his thoughts turned to memories. His acquisition of vast wealth and all the trappings that went with it— from this villa on exclusive Cap Pierre to having one of the world's most beautiful and famous faces in his bed, and all the other myriad luxuries of his life—had been only the first step in his transformation from being the unwanted, misbegotten 'embarrassing inconvenience' of his despised parents.

Parents who had conceived him in the selfish carelessness of an adulterous affair, discarding him the moment he was born, farming him out to foster parents—denying he had anything to do with them.

Well, he would prove them wrong. Prove that he could achieve by his own efforts what they had denied him.

Making himself rich—vastly so—had proved him to be the son of his philandering Greek shipping magnate father, with as much spending power as the man who had disowned him. And his marriage, he had determined, would prove himself the son of his aristocratic, adulterous French mother, enabling him to move in the same elite social circles as she, even though he was nothing more than her unwanted bastard.

Abruptly he turned away, heading back inside. Such thoughts, such memories, were always toxic—always bitter.

Down below, Nadya emerged from the water, realised Nikos was no longer watching her and, with an angry pout, seized her wrap and glowered up at the deserted balcony.

Diana sat trying not to look bored as the after-dinner speaker droned on about capital markets and fiscal policies—matters she knew nothing about and cared less. But she was attending this City livery company's formal dinner in one of London's most historic buildings simply because her partner here was an old acquaintance—Toby Masterson. And he was someone she was considering marrying.

For Toby was rich—very rich—having inherited a merchant bank. Which meant he could amply fund Greymont's restoration. He was also someone she would never fall in love with—and that was good. Diana's clear grey eyes shadowed. Good because love was dangerous. It destroyed people's happiness, ruined lives.

It had destroyed her father's happiness when her mother had deserted her doting husband for a billionaire Australian media mogul, never to be seen again. At the age of ten Diana had learnt the danger of loving someone who might not return that love—whether it was the mother who'd abandoned her without a thought, or a man who might break her heart by not loving her, as her mother had broken her father's heart.

She knew, sadly, how protective it had made him over her. She had lost her mother—he would not let her lose the home she loved so much, her beloved Greymont, the one place where she had felt safe after her mother's desertion. Life could change traumatically—the mother she'd loved had abandoned her—but Greymont was a constant, there for ever. Her home for ever.

Guilt tinged her expression now. Her father had sacrificed his own chance of finding happiness in a second marriage in order to ensure that there would never be a son to take precedence over her, to ensure that *she* would inherit Greymont.

Yet if she were to pass Greymont on to her own children she must one day marry—and, whilst she would not risk her heart in love, surely she could find a man with whom she could be on friendly terms, sufficiently compatible to make enduring a lifetime with him not unpleasant, with both of them dedicated to preserving Greymont?

A nip of anxiety caught at her expression. The trouble was, she'd always assumed she would have plenty of time to select such a man. But now, with the dire financial situation she was facing, she needed a rich husband fast. Which meant she could not afford to be fussy.

Her eyes rested on Toby as he listened to the speaker and she felt her heart sink. Toby Masterson was amiable and good-natured—but, oh, he was desperately, *desperately* dull. And, whilst she would never risk marrying a man she might fall in love with, she did at least want a man with whom the business of conceiving a child would not be…repulsive.

She gave a silent shudder at the thought of Toby's overweight body against hers, his pudgy features next to hers, trying not to be cruel, but knowing it would be gruelling for her to endure his clumsy embraces…

Could I endure that for years and years—decades?

The question hovered in her head, twisting and cringing.

She pulled her gaze away, not wanting to think such thoughts. Snapped her eyes out across the lofty banqueting hall, filled with damask-covered tables and a sea of city-folk in dinner jackets and women in evening gowns.

And suddenly, instead of a faceless mass of men in DJs, she saw that one of them had resolved into a single individual, at a table a little way away, sitting on the far side of it. A man whose dark, heavy-lidded gaze was fixed on *her*.

Nikos lounged back in his chair, long fingers curved around his brandy glass, indifferent to the after-dinner speaker who was telling him things about capital markets and fiscal policies that he knew already. Instead, his thoughts were about his personal life.

Who would he choose as his trophy wife? The woman who, now that he had achieved a vast wealth to rival that of his despised father, would be his means to achieve entry into the socially elite world of his aristocratic but heartless mother. Proving to himself, and to the world, and above all to the parents who had never cared about him, that their unwanted offspring had done fine—just fine—without them.

His brow furrowed. Marriage was supposed to be lifelong, but did he want that—even with a trophy wife? His affair with Nadya had lasted two years before boredom had set in. Would he want any longer in a marriage? Once he had got what a trophy wife offered him—his place in her world—he could do without her very well.

Certainly there would be no question of love in the relationship, for that was an emotion quite unknown to him. He had never loved Nadya, nor she him—they had merely been useful to each other. The foster couple paid to raise him had not loved him. They had not been unkind, merely uninterested, and he had no contact with them now. As for his birth parents… His mouth twisted, his eyes hardening. Had they considered their sordid adulterous affair to be about *love*?

He snapped his mind away. Went back to considering the question of his future trophy wife. First, though, he had to sever relations with Nadya, currently in New York at a fashion show. He would tell her tactfully, thanking her for the time they'd had together—which had been good, as he was the first to acknowledge—before she flew back. He would bestow upon her a lavish farewell gift—her favourite emeralds—and wish her well. Doubtless she was prepared for this moment, and would have his successor selected already.

Just as he was now planning to select the next woman in his life.

He eased his shoulders back in the chair, taking another mouthful of his cognac. He was here in London on business, attending this City function specifically for networking, and he let his dark gaze flicker out over the throng of diners, identifying those he wished to approach once the tedious after-dinner speaker was finally done.

He was on the point of lowering his brandy glass, when he halted. His gaze abruptly zeroed in on one face. A woman sitting a few tables away.

Until now his view of her had been obscured, but as other diners shifted to face the after-dinner speaker she had become visible.

His gaze narrowed assessingly. She was extraordinarily beautiful, in a style utterly removed from the fiery, dramatic features of Nadya. This woman was blonde, the hair drawn back into a French pleat as pale as her alabaster complexion, her face fine-boned, her eyes clear, wide-set, her perfect mouth enhanced with lip-gloss. She looked remote, her beauty frozen.

One phrase slid across his mind.

Ice maiden.

Another followed.

Look, but don't touch.

And immediately, instantly, that was exactly what Nikos wanted to do. To cross over to her, curve his long fingers around that alabaster face and tilt it up to his, to feel the cool satin of her pale skin beneath the searching tips of his fingers, to glide his thumbs sensually across that luscious mouth, to see those pale, expressionless eyes flare with sudden reaction, feel her iced glaze melt beneath his touch.

The intensity of the impulse scythed through him. His grip around his brandy glass tightened. Decision seared within him. A trophy wife might be next on his list of life ambitions, but that did not mean he had to seek her out immediately. He had been with Nadya for two years—no reason not to enjoy a more temporary liaison before seeking his bride.

And he had just seen the ideal woman for that role. Ideal.

With an effort, Diana sheared her gaze away, heard the speech finally ending.

'Phew!' Toby exclaimed, throwing Diana a look of apology. 'Sorry to make you endure all that,' he said.

She gave a polite smile, but in her mental vision was the face of the man who had been looking at her across the tables. The image was burning in her head.

Darkly tanned, strong features, sable hair feathering his broad forehead, high cheekbones, a blade of a nose and a mouth with a sculpted contour that somehow disturbed her—but, oh, not nearly so much as the heavy-lidded dark, dark eyes that had rested on her.

Eyes that she still felt watching her, even though she was not looking at him. Did not want to. Didn't dare to.

She felt her heart give a sudden extra beat, as if a shot of pure adrenaline had been injected into her bloodstream. Something that she was supremely un-used to—unused to handling. She was accustomed to men looking at her—but not to the way she had reacted to *this* man.

Urgently she made her eyes cling to Toby. Famil-iar, amiable Toby, with his pudgy face and portly fig-ure. In comparison with the man who'd been looking at her, poor Toby seemed pudgier and portlier than ever. Her eyes slid away, her heart sinking. She was feeling bad about what she was contemplating. Could she *really* be considering marrying him just because he was rich?

Guilt smote her that she should feel that way about him, but there it was. Had seeing that darkly disturb-ingly good-looking man just now made her realise how impossible it would be for her to marry a man like Toby? But if not Toby then who? Who could save Greymont for her?

Where can I find him? And how soon?

It was proving harder than she'd so desperately hoped, and time was running out…

Speeches finally over, the atmosphere in the ban-queting hall lightened, and there was a sense of gen-eral movement amongst the tables as diners started to mingle. Nikos was talking to his host, a City acquaintance, and casually bringing the subject around to the woman who had so piqued his interest. The ice maiden...

He nodded in her direction. 'Who's the blonde?' he asked laconically.

'I don't know her myself,' came the reply, 'but the man she's with is Toby Masterson—Masterson Dubrett, merchant bankers. Want an introduction?'

'Why not?' said Nikos.

There had been nothing in his brief perusal to indicate that the blonde's dinner partner was anything more to her—an impression confirmed as he was introduced.

'Toby Masterson—Nikos Tramontes of Tramontes Financials. Fingers in many pies—some of them might interest you and vice versa,' his host said briefly, and left them to it, heading off to talk elsewhere.

For a few minutes Nikos exchanged the kind of anodyne business talk that would interest a London merchant banker, and then he glanced at Toby Masterson's guest.

The ice maiden was not looking at him. Quite deliberately not looking at him. He was glad of it. Women who came on to him bored him. Nadya had played hard to get—she knew her own value as one of the world's most beautiful women, and was courted by many men. But he did not think the ice maiden was playing any such game—her reserve was genuine.

It made him all the more interested in her.

Expectantly he glanced at Toby Masterson, who dutifully performed the required introduction.

'Diana,' he said genially, 'this is Nikos Tramontes.'

She was forced to look at him, though her grey eyes were expressionless. Carefully expressionless.

'How do you do, Mr Tramontes?' she intoned in a cool voice. She spoke with the familiar tones of the English upper class, and only the briefest smile of courtesy indented her mouth.

Nikos gave her an equally brief courtesy smile. 'How do you do, Ms...?' He glanced at Masterson for her surname.

'St Clair,' Masterson supplied.

'Ms St Clair,' he said, his glance going back to the ice maiden.

Her face was still expressionless, but in the depths of her clear grey eyes he was sure he saw a sudden veiling, as if she were guarding herself from his perusal of her. That was good—it showed him that despite her glacial expression she was responsive to him.

Satisfied, he turned his attention back to Toby Masterson, moving their conversation on to the EU, the latest manoeuvres from Brussels, and thence on to the current state of the Greek economy.

'Does it impact *you*?' Toby Masterson was asking.

Nikos shook his head. 'Despite my name, I'm based in Monaco. I've a villa on Cap Pierre.' He glanced at Diana St Clair. 'What of you, Ms St Clair? Do you care for the South of France?'

It was a direct question, and she had to answer it. Had to look at him, engage eye contact.

'I seldom go abroad,' she replied.

Her tone still held that persistent note of not wanting to converse, and he watched her reach for her liqueur glass, raise it to her lips as if to give her something to do—something to enable her not to answer more fully. Yet her hand trembled very, very slightly as she replaced her glass, and satisfaction again bit in Nikos. The permafrost was not as deep as she wanted to convey.

'That's not surprising,' Masterson supplied jovially. 'The St Clairs have a spectacular place in the country to enjoy—Hampshire, isn't it? Greymont?' he checked. 'Eighteenth-century stately pile,' he elaborated.

Do they, indeed? thought Nikos. He looked at her with sudden deeper interest.

'Do you know Hampshire?' Toby Masterson was asking now.

'Not at all,' said Nikos, keeping his eyes on Diana St Clair. 'Greymont? Is that right?'

For the first time he saw an expression in her eyes. A flash that seemed to spear him with the intensity of the emotion behind it. It made him certain that behind the ice was a very, very different woman. A woman capable of passion.

Then it was gone, and the frost was back in her eyes. But it had left a residue. A residue that just for a moment he thought was bleakness.

'Yes,' she murmured.

He made a mental note. He would have a full dossier on her by tomorrow—Ms Diana St Clair of Greymont, Hampshire. What kind of place was it? What kind of family were the St Clairs? And just what further interest might Ms Diana St Clair have for him other than presenting him with so delectable a challenge to his seductive powers to melt an ice maiden?

His eyes flickered over her consideringly. Exquisitely beautiful and waiting to be melted into his arms, his bed... But could there be yet more to his interest in her? Could she be a candidate for something more than a fleeting affair?

Well, his investigations would reveal that.

For now, however, he had whetted his appetite—and he knew with absolute certainty that he had made the impact on her that he had intended, though she was striving not to let it show.

He turned his attention back to Masterson, taking his leave with a casual suggestion of some potential mutual business interest at an indeterminate future date.

As he strolled away his mood was good—very good indeed. With or without any deeper interest in her, the ice maiden was on the way to becoming his. But on what terms he had yet to decide.

He let his thoughts turn to how he might make his next move on her...

CHAPTER TWO

DIANA THREW HERSELF back in the taxi and heaved a sigh of pent-up relief. Safe at last.

Safe from Nikos Tramontes. From his powerfully unsettling impact on her. An impact she was not used to experiencing.

It had disturbed her profoundly. She had done her best to freeze him out, but a man that good-looking would not be accustomed to rebuff—would be used to getting his own way with women.

Well, not with me! Because I have no intention of having anything to do with him.

She shook her head, as if to clear his so disturbing image from her mind's eye. She had far more to worry about. She knew now, resignedly, that she could not face marrying Toby—but what other solution could save her beloved home?

Anxiety pressed at her—and over the next two days in London it worsened. Her bank declined to advance the level of loan required, the auction houses confirmed there was nothing left to sell to raise such a sum. So it was with little enthusiasm that she took a call from Toby.

'But it's Covent Garden. And I *know* you love opera.'

The plaintive note in Toby's voice made Diana feel bad. She owed him a gentle let-down. Reluctantly she acquiesced to his invitation—a corporate jolly for a performance of Verdi's *Don Carlo.*

But when she arrived at the Opera House she wished she had refused.

'You remember Nikos Tramontes, don't you?' Toby greeted her. 'He's our host tonight.'

Diana forced a mechanical smile to her face, concealing her dismay. With her own problems uppermost in her mind, she'd managed to start forgetting him, and the discomforting impact he'd had on her, but now suddenly he was here, as powerfully, disturbingly attractive as before.

Then she was being introduced to the other couple present. Diana recognised the man who had brought Nikos Tramontes over to their table. With him was his wife, who promptly took advantage of the three men starting to talk business to draw Diana aside.

'My, my,' she said conspiratorially, throwing an openly appraising look back at Nikos Tramontes, 'he is most definitely a handsome brute. No wonder he's been able to hold on to Nadya Serensky for so long. That and all his money, of course.'

Diana looked blank, and Louise Melmott promptly enlightened her.

'Nadya Serensky. You know—that stunning red-headed supermodel. They're quite an item.'

It was welcome news to Diana. Perhaps she'd only

been imagining that Nikos Tramontes had eyed her up at the livery dinner.

Maybe it's just me, overreacting.

Overreacting because it was so strange to encounter a man who could have such a powerfully disturbing physical impact on her. Yes, that must be it. She tried to think, as she sipped her champagne in the Crush Room, if she had ever reacted so strongly as that to any other man, and came up blank. But then, of course, she *didn't* react to men. Had schooled herself all her life not to.

The men she'd dated over the years had been good-looking, but they had always left her cold. A tepid goodnight kiss had been the most any of them had ever received. Only with one, while at university, had she resolved to see if it were possible to have a full relationship without excessive passion of any kind.

She had found that it was—for herself. But eventually not for her boyfriend. He'd found her lack of enthusiasm off-putting and had left her for another woman. It hadn't bothered her—had only confirmed how right she was to guard her heart. Losing it was so dangerous. A policy of celibacy was much wiser, much safer.

Anxiety bit at her. Except such a policy would hardly find her a husband rich enough to save Greymont. *If* she was truly still contemplating so drastic a solution.

With an inward sigh she pulled her mind away. Tomorrow she would be heading back to Greymont to go through her finances again, get the latest grim estimates for the most essential work. But for now, tonight, she would enjoy her evening at Covent Garden—a night off from her worries.

And she would not worry, either, about the presence of the oh-so-disturbing Nikos Tramontes. If he had a famous supermodel to amuse him then he would not be interested in any other women. Including herself.

As they made their way to their box she felt her anticipation rising. The orchestra was tuning up, elegant well-heeled people were taking their seats, and up in the gods the less well-heeled were packed like sardines.

Diana looked up at them slightly ruefully. The world would see her as an extremely privileged person—and she was; she knew that—but owning Greymont came with heavy responsibilities. Prime of which was stopping it from actually falling down.

But, no, she wouldn't think of her fears for Greymont. She would enjoy the evening.

'Allow me.'

Nikos Tramontes's deep, faintly accented voice beside her made her start. He drew her chair back, allowing her to take her seat, which she did with a rustling of her skirts as he seated himself behind her. Louise Melmott sat beside her at the front of the box.

His eyes rested on the perfect profile of the woman whose presence here tonight he had specifically engineered in order to pursue his interest in her. An interest that the dossier he had ordered to be compiled on her had indicated he must show. Because she might very well indeed prove suitable for far more than a mere fleeting seduction.

Diana St Clair, it seemed, was possessed of more than the exquisite glacial beauty that had so caught his attention the other evening. She was also possessed of exactly the right background and attributes to suit his purposes. Best of all about Ms Diana St Clair was her inheritance—her eighteenth-century country estate—and the fact that it *was* her inheritance, bringing with it all the elite social background that such ownership conferred.

An old county family—not titled, but anciently armigerous—possessing crests and coats of arms and all the heraldic flourishes that went with that status. With landed property and position, centuries of intermarriage with other such families, including the peerage. A complex web of kinship and connection running like a web across the upper classes, binding them together, impenetrable to outsiders.

Except by one means only…

Marriage.

His eyes rested on her, their expression veiled. Would Diana St Clair be his trophy wife?

It was a tempting prospect. As tempting as Diana St Clair herself.

He sat back to enjoy further contemplation of this woman who might achieve what he now most wanted from life.

* * *

To Diana's relief, the dramatic sweep of Verdi's music carried her away, despite her burning consciousness that Nikos Tramontes was sitting so close to her, and as she surfaced for the first interval it was to be ushered with his other guests back to the Crush Room for the first course of their champagne supper.

The conversation was led mainly by Louise Melmott, who knew the opera and its doubtful relationship to actual history.

'The real Don Carlos of Spain was probably insane,' the other woman said cheerfully, as they helped themselves to the delicacies on offer. 'And there's no evidence he was in love with his father the King's, wife!'

'I can see why Verdi rewrote history,' Diana observed. 'A tragic, thwarted love affair sounds far more romantically operatic.'

She was doing her best to be a good guest—especially since she knew Toby had no interest in opera, so she needed to emphasise her own enthusiasm.

'Elisabeth de Valois was another man's wife. There is nothing romantic about adultery.'

Nikos Tramontes's voice was harsh, and Diana looked at him in surprise.

'Well, opera is hardly realistic—and surely for a woman like the poor Queen, trapped in a loveless marriage, especially when she'd thought she was going to be married to the King's son, not the King himself—surely one can only feel pity for her plight?'

Dark eyes rested on her. '*Can* one?'

Was there sarcasm in the way he replied? Diana felt herself colouring slightly. She had only intended a fairly light remark.

The conversation moved on, but Diana felt stung. As if she'd voted personally in favour of adultery. She felt Nikos Tramontes's eyes resting on her, their expression masked. There seemed to be a brooding quality about him suddenly, at odds with the urbane, self-assured manner he'd demonstrated so far.

Well, it was nothing to do with her—and nor was Nikos Tramontes. She would not be seeing him again after this evening.

It was to her distinct annoyance, therefore, that when the long opera finally ended and she had bade goodnight to Toby, making sure she told him she was heading back to Hampshire the next day, she discovered that somehow Nikos Tramontes was at her side as she left the Opera House. It was a mild but damp night, and his car was clearly hovering at the kerb.

'Allow me to offer you a lift,' he said. His voice was smooth.

Diana stiffened. 'Thank you, but a taxi will be fine.'

'You won't find one closer than the Strand, and it is about to rain,' he returned blandly.

Then he was guiding her forward, opening the rear passenger door for her. Annoyed, but finding it hard to object without making an issue of it, Diana got in. Reluctantly she gave the name of the hotel she and

her father had always used on their rare visits to the
capital, and the car moved off.

In the confines of the back seat, separated from
the driver by a glass divide, Nikos Tramontes seemed
even more uncomfortably close than he had in the
opera box. His long legs stretched out into the foot-
well.

'I'm glad you enjoyed this evening,' he began. He
paused minutely. 'Perhaps you'd like to come with
me to another performance some time? Unless you've
seen all this season's productions already?'

There was nothing more than mild enquiry in his
bland voice, but Diana felt herself tense. Dismay filled
her. He was making a move on her after all, despite
the presence in his life of Nadya Serensky. Her hopes
that her disturbing reaction to him were not returned
plummeted.

'I'm afraid not,' she said, giving a quick shake of
her head.

'You haven't seen them all?' he queried.

She shook her head again, making herself look
at him. His face was half shadowed in the dim interior, with the only light coming from the street lights
and shop windows as they made their way along the
Strand towards Trafalgar Square.

'That isn't what I meant,' she said. She made her
voice firm.

His response was to lift an eyebrow. 'Masterson?'
he challenged laconically.

She gave a quick shake of her head. 'No, but…'

'Yes?' he prompted, as she trailed off.

Diana took a breath, clasping her hands in her lap. She made her voice composed, but decisive. 'I spend very little time in London, Mr Tramontes, and because of that it would be…pointless to accept any…ah…further invitation from you. For whatever purpose.'

She said no more. It struck her that for him to have sounded so very disapproving of a fictional case of adultery in the plot of Don Carlos was more than a little hypocritical of him, given that he'd just asked her out. Clearly he was not averse to playing away himself, she thought acidly.

She saw him ease his shoulders back into the soft leather of his seat. Saw a sardonic smile tilt at his mouth. Caught a sudden scent of his aftershave, felt the closeness of his presence.

'Do you *know* my purpose?' he murmured, with a quizzical, faintly mocking look in his dark eyes.

She pressed her mouth tightly. 'I don't need to, Mr Tramontes. I'm simply making it clear that since I don't spend much time in London I won't have any opportunities to go to the opera, whomever I might go with.'

'You're returning to Hampshire?'

She nodded. 'Yes. Indefinitely. I don't know when I shall be next in town,' she said, wanting to make crystal-clear her unavailability.

He seemed to accept her answer. 'I quite understand,' he said easily.

She felt a sense of relief go through her. He was backing off—she could tell. For all that, she still felt a level of agitation that was unsettling. It came simply from his physical closeness. She was aware that her heart rate had quickened. It was unnerving…

Then, thankfully, the car was turning off Piccadilly and drawing up outside the hotel where she was staying. The doorman came forward to open her door and she was soon climbing out, trying not to hurry. Making her voice composed once more.

'Goodnight, Mr Tramontes. Thank you so much for a memorable evening at the opera, and thank you for this lift now.'

She disappeared inside the haven of the hotel.

From the car, Nikos watched her go. It was the kind of old-fashioned but upmarket hotel that well-bred provincials patronised when forced to come to town, and doubtless the St Clairs had been patronising it for generations.

His eyes narrowed slightly as his car moved off, heading back to his own hotel—far more fashionable and flashy than Diana St Clair's. Had she turned down his invitation on account of Nadya? He'd heard Louise Melmott say her name. If so, that was all to the good. It showed him that Diana St Clair was… *particular* about the men she associated with.

He had not cared for her apparent tolerance of the adultery in the plot of *Don Carlos*, but it did not seem that she carried that over into real life. It was essential that she did not.

No wife of mine will indulge in adultery—no wife of mine, however upper crust her background, will be anything like my mother! Anything at all—

Wife? Was he truly thinking of Diana St Clair in such a light?

And, if he were, what might persuade her to agree?

What could thaw that chilly reserve of hers?

What will make her receptive to me?

Whatever it was, he would find it—and use it.

He sat back, considering his thoughts, as his car merged into the late-night London traffic.

Greymont was as beautiful as ever—especially in the sunshine, which helped to disguise how the stonework was crumbling and the damp was getting in. The lead roof that needed replacing was invisible behind the parapet, and—

A wave of deep emotion swept through Diana. How could Gerald possibly imagine she might actually sell Greymont? It meant more to her than anything in the world. Anything or anyone. St Clairs had lived here for three hundred years, made their home here—of *course* she could not sell it. Each generation held it in trust for the next.

Her eyes shadowed. Her father had entrusted it to *her*, had ensured—at the price of putting aside any hopes of his own for a happier, less heart-sore second marriage—that *she* inherited. She had lost her mother—he had ensured she should not lose her home as well.

So for her to give it up now, to let it go to strangers, would be an unforgivable betrayal of his devotion to her, his trust in her. She could not do it. Whatever she had to do—she would do it. She *must*.

As she walked indoors, her footsteps echoing on the marble floor, she looked at the sweeping staircase soaring to the upper floors, at the delicate Adam mouldings in the alcoves and the equally delicate painted ceilings—both in need of attention—and the white marble fireplace, chipped now, in too many places. A few remaining family portraits by undistinguished artists were on the walls ascending the staircase, all as familiar to her as her own body.

Upstairs in her bedroom, she crossed to the window, throwing open the sash to gaze out over the gardens and the park beyond. An air of unkemptness might prevail, but the level lawns, the ornamental stone basin with its now non-functioning fountain, the pathways and the pergolas, marching away to where the ha-ha divided the formal gardens from the park, were all as lovely as they always had been. As dear and precious.

A fierce sense of protectiveness filled her. She breathed deeply of the fresh country air, then slid the window shut, noticing that it was sticking more than ever, its paint flaking—another sign of damp getting in. She could see another patch of damp on her ceiling too, and frowned.

Whilst her father had been so ill not even routine maintenance work had been done on the house, let alone anything more intensive. It would have disturbed him too much with noise and dust, and the structural survey she'd commissioned after he'd died had revealed problems even worse than she had feared or her father had envisaged.

A new roof, dozens of sash windows in need of extensive repair or replacement, rotting floorboards, collapsing chimneys, the ingress of damp, electrical rewiring, re-plumbing, new central heating needed— the list went on and on. And then there was all the decorative work, from repainting ceilings to mending tapestries to conserving curtains and upholstery.

More and yet more to do.

And that was before she considered the work that the outbuildings needed! Bowing walls, slate roofs deteriorating, cobbles to reset… A never-ending round. Even before a start was made on the overgrown gardens.

She felt her shoulders sag. So much to be done— all costing so, *so* much. She gave a sigh, starting to unpack her suitcase. Staff had been reduced to the minimum—the Hudsons, and the cleaners up from the village, plus a gardener and his assistant. It was just as well that her father had preferred a very quiet life, even if that *had* contributed to his wife's discontent. And he had become increasingly reclusive after her desertion.

It had suited Diana, though, and she'd been happy to help him write the St Clair family history, acting as secretary for his correspondence with the network of family connections, sharing his daily walks through the park, being the chatelaine of Greymont in her mother's absence.

Any socialising had been with other families like theirs in the county, such as their neighbours, Sir John Bartlett and his wife, her father's closest friends.

She herself had been more active, visiting old school and university friends around the country as they gradually married and started families, meeting up with them in London from time to time. But she was no party animal, preferring dinner parties, or going to the theatre and opera, either with girlfriends or those carefully selected men she allowed to squire her around—those who accepted she was not interested in romance and was completely unresponsive to all men.

Into her head, with sudden flaring memory, stabbed the image of the one man who had disproved that comforting theory.

Angrily, she pushed it away. It was irrelevant, her ridiculous reaction to Nikos Tramontes! She would never be seeing him again—and she had far more urgent matters to worry about.

Taking a breath, anxiety clenching her stomach, she went downstairs and settled at her father's desk in the library. In her absence mail had accumulated, and with a resigned sigh she started to open it. None of it would be good news, she knew that—more unaffordable estimates for the essential repairs to Greymont. She felt her heart squeeze, and fear bite in her throat.

Somehow she *had* to get the money she needed.

But not by marrying Toby Masterson. She could not bring herself to spend the rest of her life with him.

She felt a prickle of shame. It had not been fair even to think of him merely as a solution to her problems.

Wearily, she reached for her writing pad. She'd have to pen a careful letter—thanking him for taking her out in London, implying that that was all there was to it.

As she made a start, though, it was quite another face that intruded into her inner vision, quite different from Toby's pudgy features. A face that was dramatic in its looks, with dark eyes that set her pulse beating faster—

She pushed it from her. Even if Nikos Tramontes were *not* involved with his supermodel girlfriend, all a man like that would be after would be some kind of dalliance—something to amuse him, entertain him while he was in London.

And what use is that to me?

None. None at all.

Nikos slowly made his way along the avenue of chestnut trees, avoiding the many potholes as Greymont gradually came into view.

With a white stucco eighteenth-century façade, a central block with symmetrical wings thrown out, its aspect was open, but set on a slight elevation, with extensive gardens and grounds seamlessly blending into farmland. The whole was framed by ornamental woodland. A classic stately home of the English upper classes.

Memory jabbed at him, cruel and stabbing. Of another home of another nation's upper class. A chateau deep in the heart of Normandy, built of creamy Caen stone, with turrets at the corners in the French style.

He'd driven up to the front doors. Had been received.

But not welcomed.

'You will have to leave. My husband will be home soon. He must not find you here—'

There had been no warmth in the voice, no embrace from the elegant, couture-clad figure, no opening of her arms to him. Nothing but rejection.

'That is all you have to say to me?'

That had been his question, his demand.

Her lips had tightened. *'You must leave,'* she'd said again, not answering his question.

He had swept a glance around the room, with its immaculate décor, its priceless seventeenth-century landscapes on the walls, the exquisite Louis Quinze furniture. *This* was what she had chosen. *This* was what she had valued. And she had been perfectly willing, to pay the price demanded for it. The price *he* had paid for it.

Bitterness had filled him then—and an even stronger emotion that he would not name, would deny with steely resolve that he had ever felt. It filled him again now, a sudden acid rush in his veins.

With an effort, he let it drain out of him as he drew his powerful car to a momentary halt, the better to survey the scene before him.

Yes—what he was seeing satisfied him. More than satisfied him. Greymont, the ancestral home of the St Clairs, and all that came with it would serve his purpose excellently. But it was not just the physical possession he wanted—that was not what this visit

was about. Had he wished. he could easily have purchased such a place for himself, but that would not
have given him what he was set upon achieving.

His smile tightened. He knew just how to achieve
what he wanted. What would make Diana St Clair
receptive to him. Knew exactly what she wanted
most—needed most. And he would offer it to her.
On a plate.

His gaze still fixed on his goal, he headed towards
it.

CHAPTER THREE

'MR *TRAMONTES*?'

Diana stared blankly as Hudson conveyed the information about her totally unexpected visitor. What on earth was Nikos Tramontes doing here at Greymont?

Bemused, and with an uneasy flutter in her stomach, she walked into the library. She found her uninvited guest perusing the walls of leather-bound books, and as he turned at her entrance she felt an unwelcome jolt to her heart-rate.

It had been a week since she'd left London, but seeing his tall, commanding figure again instantly brought back the evening she'd spent at Covent Garden. Unlike on the two previous occasions she'd set eyes on him, this time he was in a suit, and the dark charcoal of the material, the pristine white of his shirt, and the discreet navy blue tie, made him every bit as eye-catching as he had been in evening dress.

It annoyed her that she should feel that sudden kick in her pulse again as she approached. She fought to suppress it, and failed.

'Ms St Clair.' He strode forward, reaching out his hand.

Numbly, she let him take hers and give it a quick, businesslike shake.

'I'm sorry to call unannounced,' he went on, his manner still businesslike, 'but there is a matter I would like to discuss with you that will be of mutual benefit to us both.'

He looked at her, his expression expectant.

Blankly, she went and sat down on the well-worn leather sofa by the fireplace, and watched him move to do likewise. He took her father's armchair, and a slight bristle of resentment went through her. She leant over to ring the ancient bell-pull beside the mantel and, when Hudson duly appeared, asked for coffee to be served.

When they were left alone again, she looked directly at her unexpected visitor. 'I really can't imagine, Mr Tramontes, that there is anything that could be of mutual benefit to us.'

Surely, for heaven's sake, he was not going to try and proposition her again? She devoutly hoped not.

He smiled, crossing one long leg over the other. It was a proprietorial gesture, and it put her hackles up. The entrance of Hudson with the coffee tray was a welcome diversion, and she busied herself pouring them both a cup, only glancing at Nikos Tramontes to ask how he took his coffee.

'Black, no sugar,' he said briskly, and took the cup she proffered.

But he did not drink from it. Instead, he swept his

gaze around the high-ceilinged, book-lined room, then brought it back to Diana.

'This is an exceptionally fine house you have, Ms St Clair,' he said. 'I can see why you won't sell.'

She started, whole body tensing. What on *earth*? How dared Nikos Tramontes make such a remark to her. It was *none* of his business.

He saw her expression and gave a smile that had a caustic twist to it. 'It wasn't that hard,' he said gently, not letting her drop her outraged gaze, 'to discover the circumstances of your inheritance. And I have eyes in my head. I may not be that familiar with English country houses, but a pot-holed drive, masonry that is crumbling below the roofline, grounds that could do with several more gardeners...'

He took a mouthful of coffee, setting the cup aside on the table her father had used to lay his daily newspaper on. Looked at her directly again.

'It makes sense of your interest in Toby Masterson,' he told her. 'A man with a merchant bank at his disposal.'

Again, outrage seethed in Diana—even more fiercely. Her voice was icy. 'Mr Tramontes, I really think—'

He held up a hand to silence her. As if, she thought stormily, she was some unruly office junior.

'Hear me out,' he said.

He paused a moment, studying her. She was dressed casually, in dark green well-cut trousers and a paler green sweater, with her hair caught back in a clip, no jewellery, and no make-up he could discern—a world away from the muted elegance of her evening dress.

But her pale, breathtaking beauty still had the same immediate powerful impact on him as it had when she'd first caught his eye. Her current unconcealed outrage only accentuated his response.

'I understand your predicament,' he said.

There was sympathy in his voice, and it made her suspicious. Her expression was shuttered, her mouth set. Her own coffee completely ignored.

'And I have a potential solution for you,' he went on.

His eyes never left her face, and there was something in their long-lashed dark regard that made it difficult to meet them. But meet them she did—even if it took an effort to appear as composed as she wanted to be.

He took her silence for assent, and continued.

'What I am about to put to you, Ms St Clair, is a solution that will be a familiar one to you, with your ancestry. I'm sure that not a few of your forebears opted for a similar solution. Though these days, fortunately, the solution can be a lot less…perhaps *irreversible* is the correct term.'

He reached for his coffee again. Took a leisurely mouthful and replaced the cup. Looked at her once more. She had neutralised her expression, but that was to be expected. Once he had put his cards on the table she would either have him shown the door—or she would agree to what he wanted.

'You wish—extremely understandably—to retain your family property. However, it's quite evident that a very substantial sum of money is going to be required—a sum that, as I'm sure you are punishingly aware, given the current level of death duties and the exceptionally high cost of conservation work on listed historic houses, is going to stretch you. Very possibly beyond your limits. Certainly beyond your comfort zone.'

Her expression was stony, giving nothing away. That didn't bother him. It made him think how statuesque her beauty was. How much it appealed to him. The contrast of her chilly ice maiden impassivity with Nadya's hot-blooded outbursts was entirely in Diana St Clair's favour. She was as unlike Nadya as a woman could be—and not, he thought with satisfaction, just in respect of the ice maiden quality, but in so much more—all of which was supremely useful to him.

'As I say, you've clearly already considered—and rejected—Toby Masterson as a solution to your problem, but now I invite you to consider an alternative candidate.'

He paused. A deliberate, telling pause. His eyes held hers like hooks.

'Myself,' he said.

Diana's intake of breath was audible. It scraped through her throat and seemed to dry her lungs to ashes.

'Are you *mad*?' came from her.

'Not in the least,' was his unruffled reply. 'This is what I propose.' His mouth tightened a moment, then he went on. 'I should make it clear immediately, however, that my relationship with Nadya Serensky is at an end. She was a woman I wanted two years ago—now I want something, and some*one*, quite different. *You*, Ms St Clair, suit my requirements perfectly. And I,' he continued, ignoring the mounting look of disbelief on her face, 'suit *your* requirements perfectly, too.'

She opened her mouth to speak, to protest, but no words came. What words could possibly come in response to such a brazen, unbelievable announcement? He was continuing to talk in that same cool manner, as if he were discussing the weather, and she could only listen to what he said. Even while she stared at him blankly.

'What I want now, at this stage of my life,' he was saying—perfectly calmly, perfectly casually, 'is a wife. Nadya was quite unsuitable for that role. You, however...'

His dark eyes rested on her, unreadable and opaque, and yet somehow seeing right into her, she felt with a hollowing of her stomach.

'You are perfect for that part. As I,' he finished, 'am perfect for you.'

She could only stare, frozen with disbelief. And with another emotion that was trying to snake around her stunned mind.

'We would each,' he said, 'provide the other with what we currently want.' He glanced once more around the library, then back to her. 'I want to be part of the world you inhabit—the world of country houses like this, and those who were born to them. Oh, I could quite easily buy such a house, but that

would not serve my purpose. I would be an outsider.
A *parvenu*.'

His voice was edged, and he felt the familiar wash
of bitterness in his veins, but she was simply staring at
him, with a stunned expression on her beautiful face.

'That will not do for me,' he said. 'What I want,
therefore, is a wife from that world, who will make
me a part of it by marrying her, so that I am accepted.'
Again, his voice tightened as he continued. 'As for
what *you* would gain…' His expression changed. 'I
am easily able to afford the work that needs to be done
to ensure the fabric of this magnificent edifice is repaired and restored to the condition it should enjoy.
So you see…' he gave his faint smile '…how suitable
we are for each other?'

She found her voice—belatedly—her words faint
as she forced them out.

'I cannot believe you are serious. We have met
precisely twice. You're a complete stranger to me.
And I to you.'

He gave the slightest shrug of his broad shoulders.
'That can easily be remedied. I am perfectly prepared
for our engagement to provide sufficient time to set
you at your ease with me.'

He reached to take up his coffee cup again, lev-
elled his unreadable gaze on her.

'I am not suggesting,' he continued, 'a lifetime
together. Two years at the most—possibly less. Sufficient for each of us to get what we want from the
other. That is, after all, one of the distinct advantages
of our times—unlike your forebears, who might have

made similar mutually advantageous matches, we are free to dissolve our marriage of our own volition and go our separate ways thereafter.'

He took another draught of his coffee, finishing it and setting down the cup. He looked directly at her.

'Well? What is your answer?'

She swallowed. There was a maelstrom in her head: thoughts and counter-thoughts, conflicting emotions. Swirling about chaotically. This couldn't be real, could it? This almost complete stranger, sitting here suggesting they marry?

Marry so I can save Greymont—

She felt a hollowing inside her. That had been exactly what she herself had contemplated—had told Gerald Langley that she would do. She had seriously contemplated it with Toby, then balked at making a life-long commitment to a man she would never otherwise have considered marrying.

But Nikos Tramontes only wants two years.

Two brief years of her life.

Sharply, she looked at him.

'You say no longer than two years?'

He nodded, concealing an inner sense of triumph. That she had asked the question showed she was giving his offer serious consideration. That she was tempted.

'I think that will suffice, don't you?'

It would for him—he was confident of that. Not just because when they parted he would be secure in the social position that marriage to her would give him, but because he knew from his liaison with Nadya that he was unlikely to be bored with the woman in his life before then. For two years, therefore, having Diana St Clair in his life, his bed, would be perfectly acceptable.

He let his gaze rest on her, absorbing her pristine beauty, the pallor in her cheeks from her reaction to his proposition. She was still looking dazed, but no longer outraged. Again, triumph surged in him. He knew he was most definitely drawing her in.

'Well?' he prompted.

'I need time,' she said weakly. 'I can't just—' She broke off, unable to say more, feeling as if a tornado had just scooped her up and whirled her about.

'Of course,' Nikos conceded smoothly.

He got to his feet. His six-foot-plus height seemed to overpower her.

'Think it over. I'm flying to Zurich tomorrow, but I will be back in the UK at the end of next week. You can give me your answer then. In the meantime, if you have any further questions feel free to text or email me.'

She watched him extract a business card and lay it on her father's desk before turning back to her.

Suddenly, he smiled. 'Don't look so shocked, Diana. It could work perfectly for both of us. A marriage of convenience—people made them all the time in the past. They still do, even if they don't admit it.'

He turned on his heel, leaving her sitting staring after him as he left the room. She heard his swift footsteps, the front door opening and closing again. The sound of a car starting. Her heart was pounding like a hammer inside her. And it wasn't just because of the bombshell he'd dropped in her lap.

When he smiles and calls me by my name...

She felt her pulse give a quiver, and deep inside her she felt danger roil. For reasons she could not understand Nikos Tramontes, of all the men she had ever known, seemed to possess an ability to...to *disturb* her. To make her hyper-aware of his masculinity. Of her own femininity. She didn't know where it was coming from, or why—she only knew it was dangerous.

I don't want to react to him like that—I don't want to!

Her features contorted. Nikos Tramontes had walked into her life out of nowhere and put down in front of her what could be the best hope she had of getting exactly what she wanted—the means to save Greymont. As easily and as painlessly as it was possible to do so outside of a lottery win.

Yes, he was a complete stranger—but, as he'd said, they could get to know each other during their engagement. Yes, his announcement had initially shocked her. But, as he'd also said, such marriages for mutual advantage had been perfectly unexceptional to her ancestors. And theirs would be brief—a year or two at most. Not the life-long commitment that Toby would have required...

And yet for all that she heard a voice wail in her head.

Why can't he look like Toby? Overweight and

pug-faced! That would be so, so much better! So much safer.

So much safer than the dangerous quickening of her blood that came whenever she thought of Nikos Tramontes.

Deliberately, she silenced her fear. Dismissing it. There was no need for such anxieties. None! That quickening of her blood was irrelevant—completely irrelevant. It had nothing to do with what Nikos Tramontes was offering her.

The formality of a marriage of convenience, for outward show only—a dispassionate, temporary union to provide him with an assured entrée into her world and her with the means to preserve her inheritance. Nothing else—nothing that had anything to do with that quickening of her pulse.

It was because she owned Greymont and came with the social position and connections he wanted to acquire that he was interested in her. Nothing more than that. Oh, he would want her to grace his arm, be an ornament for him—that was understandable. But that would be in public. In private their relationship would be cordial, but fundamentally, she reassured herself, it would be little more than a business arrangement at heart. He got a society wife—she got Greymont restored. Mutually beneficial.

We would be associates. That's a good word for it.

With a little start she realised she was giving his extraordinary proposition serious consideration.

Her mind reeled again.

Could she really do this? Accept his offer—use it to save Greymont?

It was all she could think about as the days went by. Days spent in visits from the architect, and from the specialist companies that would undertake the careful restoration and conservation work on Greymont that would have to be carried out in accordance to the strict building regulations for historic listed buildings, adding to the complexity—and the cost.

With every passing day she could feel the temptation to accept what Nikos was offering her coiling itself like a serpent around her. Tightening its grip with every coil.

Nikos settled himself into a seat in first class. His mood was good—very good. His decision to select Diana St Clair as the means of achieving his life's second imperative goal might have been made impulsively, but he'd always trusted his instincts. They'd never failed him in business yet, enabling his rise to riches to be as meteoric as it had been steep.

A faint frown furrowed his brow as he accepted a glass of champagne from the attentive stewardess.

But marriage is not a business decision...

He shook the thought from him. His liaison with Nadya hadn't been a business decision, but it had proved highly beneficial to both of them while it had lasted, with each of them gaining substantially from it. There was no reason why his time with Diana St Clair should not do likewise. As well as gaining the restoration of her home, she would gain an attentive husband and a *very* attentive lover.

What more could she—or he—want?

Certainly not love.

His mouth twisted. Love was of no interest to him. He'd never known it, did not want it. And nor, clearly, did Diana St Clair, or she would have sent him packing when he'd set out his proposal in front of her. But she hadn't—and she would accept it, he knew, his expression changing to one of confident assurance.

What he was offering suited her perfectly. And not just as the means to save her home. On a much more personal level too. Oh, she might not yet realise that her inner ice maiden had finally met a challenge it could not freeze off, but when the time came—and come it would!—she would accept from him all the exquisite sensual pleasure that he would ensure she experienced, all the pleasure that he was so hotly anticipating for himself.

It would be his gift to her—opening the door for her to accept the admiration and desire of men at last. Frozen as she was within, he would ignite within her that flare of sensual awareness he'd seen so briefly, so revealingly in her eyes when he'd first looked upon her.

He would not hurry her—he would give her time to get used to him—but in the end… His smile deepened and he took a mouthful of champagne, easing his shoulders as an image of her pale, exquisite beauty formed in his mind's eye, lingering over the fine-boned features, the silken line of her mouth.

In the end she would thaw.

And melt into his waiting arms.

Diana stared at the vast bouquet of exotic, highly scented lilies that sat on the Boule table in the hall, fragrancing the air. Then she stared down at the cheque she was holding in her slightly shaking hands, and the note accompanying it.

An advance, sent in good faith.

She stared at the numbers on the cheque. A quarter of a million pounds. She felt her lungs tighten. So much money—

With a stifled noise in her throat she marched back into her office. But the scent of the lilies was in her nostrils still. Beguiling. Enticing.

Can I do it? Marry Nikos Tramontes?

The cheque in her hand demanded an answer. Accept or reject it. Accept or reject the man who'd signed it.

The phone on her desk rang, startling her. It was her architect, politely, tactfully enquiring whether she was yet in a position to set a start date for the work that needed to be done. Work that could not start without Nikos to pay for it.

Her hand clenched, her signet ring with the St Clair crest on her little finger catching on the mahogany surface of the desk. Emotion bit into her, forcing a decision. The decision she had to make *now*. Could postpone no longer. If she did not restore Greymont it would decay into ruins or she would have to sell. Either way, it would be lost.

I can't be the St Clair who loses Greymont. I can't betray my father's devotion and sacrifice. I can't!

The offer that Nikos Tramontes had put in front of her was the best she could ever hope to find. It was a gift from heaven.

Nothing else can save Greymont.

She could feel her heart thumping in her chest, her mouth drying, suddenly, at the enormity of what she was doing.

It will be all right—it will be all right...

She heard the words in her head, calming her, and she clung to them urgently.

Slowly—very, very slowly—she breathed out. Then she spoke. 'Yes,' she said to her architect. 'I think we can now make a start.'

CHAPTER FOUR

THE WEDDING VENUE WAS the ballroom of an historic London hotel, with impeccable upper-crust ambience and timelessly stylish art deco décor, and it was packed with people.

Apart from the guests who were Nikos's business acquaintances, Diana had rounded up everyone from her own circles whom Nikos Tramontes was marrying her in order to meet: those people who represented upper-class English society, based on centuries of land ownership and 'old money', who had all gone to school together, intermarried over the years, and would socialise together for ever. It was a closed club, open only to those born into it. Or to those who, like her new husband, had married into it.

She was glad so many had accepted her invitation— it made her feel she was definitely keeping her side of the bargain she'd struck with the man she was marrying. He wanted a society wife—she was making sure he got one, in return for funding the repairs now actively underway at Greymont.

The ongoing work had been her main preoccupation during the three months of their engagement, but she had made time to meet up with Nikos whenever he was in London, including attending a lavish engagement party at his newly purchased town house in Knightsbridge. The fact that his business affairs seemed to require his continuous travel around the globe suited her fine.

All the same, he'd taken pains to allow her to get used to him, to come to terms with being his fiancée, just as he'd promised he would. He'd taken her out and about to dinner, to the theatre and the opera, and to meet some of her friends or his business acquaintances.

He was no longer a stranger by any means. And, although she had been unable to banish that unwanted hyperawareness of his compelling masculinity that made her so constantly self-conscious about him, she had, nevertheless, become far easier in his company. More comfortable being with him. His manners were polished, his conversation intelligent, and there was nothing about him to make her regret her decision to accept marriage to him as a solution for Greymont.

Becoming engaged to Nikos had proved a lot more easy than she had feared. He'd certainly set aside her lingering disquiet that her disturbing awareness of his sexual magnetism might cause a problem. He seemed oblivious to it, and she was grateful. It would be embarrassing, after all, if a man to whom she was making a hard-headed marriage of convenience were to be inconvenienced by a fiancée who trembled at his touch.

Not that he did touch her. Apart from socially conventional contact, such as taking her arm or guiding her forward, which she was studiously trying to inoculate herself against, he never laid a finger on her. Not even a peck on the cheek.

It was ironic, she thought wryly, that her friends all assumed her sudden engagement was a *coup de foudre*...

She'd let Toby Masterson think so, out of kindness for him, and he'd said sadly, 'I could tell you were smitten, from the off,' before he wished her well.

The only dissenting voice against her engagement had come from Gerald, the St Clair family lawyer.

'Diana, are you sure this is what you want to do?' he'd asked warningly.

'Yes,' she'd said decisively, 'it is.'

As she'd answered that old saying had come into her head. *'Take what you want,' says God. 'Take it and pay for it.'*

She'd shaken it from her. All she was paying was two years of her life. She could afford that price. Two years in which to grace the arm of Nikos Tramontes in their marriage of convenience, a perfectly civil and civilised arrangement. She had no problem with that.

And no problem with standing in the receiving line beside him now, greeting their guests as his wife. She stood there smiling, saying all that was proper for the occasion, and continued to smile throughout the reception.

Only when, finally, she sank back into the plush seat of the vintage car that was to take them to the airport, from where they would fly off on their honeymoon in the Gulf—where Nikos had business affairs to see to—did she feel as if she'd come offstage after a bravura performance.

She could finally relax.

'Relieved it's all over?'

Nikos's deep voice at her side, made her glance at him.

'Yes.' She nodded decisively. 'And I'm glad it all went flawlessly.'

He smiled at her. 'But then, you were flawless yourself.'

'Thank you,' she said, acknowledging his compliment.

She was getting used to his smiles now. Making herself get used to them. Just as she would make herself get used to the fact that he was her husband for the time being. Theirs might be a marriage of convenience, but it could be perfectly amiable for all that. Indeed, there was no reason why it shouldn't be. The more time she spent with him, the easier it would get.

Even on a honeymoon that was actually a business trip.

'It's been pretty strenuous,' she went on now, easing her feet out of the low-heeled court shoes that went with her cream silk 'going away' outfit— considerably more comfortable than those that had gone with her thirties-style, ivory satin bias-cut wedding dress, which had been four-inch heeled sandals. 'But, yes, I think I can agree it's all gone extremely well. And, of course—' and now there was real warmth in her voice '—the work at Greymont is making wonderful progress. I can't thank you enough for expediting matters in that respect!'

'Well, that *is* my contribution,' he agreed.

It had been a long day, and she'd been on the go from the moment she'd woken in the bridal suite at the hotel, ready to receive the ministrations of hair stylists and make-up artists, to this moment of relative relaxation now, and maybe that accounted for the tightening of her throat, the rush of emotion in her voice.

'It means so much to me—restoring Greymont. It's my whole world. '

Was there a flicker in his eyes? A sudden shadowing? But he said nothing, only smiled before getting out his phone with a murmured apology about checking emails.

She let him get on with it. He was a businessman. And global business ran twenty-four-seven. It didn't stop for weddings.

Or honeymoons.

Yet when they arrived in the Gulf—Diana having managed to get some sleep during the flight—it was to discover that the incredibly lavish hotel they were staying at was most definitely putting the honeymoon into their arrival with a capital H.

As they were conducted to their suite by a personal butler, Diana could not suppress a gasp. The walls seemed to be made of gold, as did most of the furniture, a vast sweep of glass gave a view out over the vista beyond, and the floor looked to be priceless marble. Huge bouquets of red roses stood on just about every surface, scenting the air richly.

'Oh, my goodness…' she said weakly.

Did she really lean slightly against Nikos, half in weariness, half in amazement at the utterly over-the-top gilded lavishness of their surroundings? She didn't know—knew only that for a moment his strength seemed to be supporting her. And then he was leading her forward, to where their butler was opening a bottle of vintage champagne.

'Is it giving you ideas for improving the décor at Greymont?'

Nikos's low voice was at her ear. She cast him a look, then realised that there was a hint of humour at his mouth and in his eyes. She felt a strange flutter deep inside her. Even though she was getting used to his smiles, he should not smile at her like that. Not so intimately. Not in a marriage like theirs—a marriage in which intimacy was not in the terms and conditions.

'It's perfect for *here*,' she allowed.

She took the glass of champagne proffered to her and Nikos did likewise, dismissing the butler.

He raised his glass. 'Well, Mrs Tramontes, shall we drink a toast to our marriage?'

That smile was still in his eyes, but now she was more composed as she met his gaze.

'Definitely,' she said brightly, lifting her glass to his.

It was odd to hear him call her that. She'd heard it a few times at the wedding reception, but it hadn't seemed real then. Now, coming from Nikos, it did.

Well, yes, on the surface I suppose it is *real, in the legal sense. But it's not* really *real—it's simply...*

Convenient.

That was what it was. Convenient for both of them. Almost a kind of business partnership.

Mutually beneficial, perfectly amicable.

She clinked her glass against his lightly. Smiled back at him. Brightly, civilly, cheerfully. OK, she wasn't yet *totally* used to being in his company, but the next few days would see to that.

She just had to get used to him, that was all.

'To us...'

Nikos's voice was deep, but if she'd thought for a second she'd heard something in it that smacked of some kind of intimacy, well, she was sure she was mistaken. He was, she reminded herself, a formidably attractive man, and he would have an impact on any woman without even intending to.

'To us,' she returned, and took a dutiful mouthful.

Nikos slid open the door to the huge balcony and they stepped out to take in the vista of the hotel's gardens and azure swimming pools, and the glittering waters of the Gulf beyond.

She gave a sigh of pleasure and leant against the glass balcony rail. Nikos moved beside her, not too close, but almost in a companionable fashion, looking down with her, taking in the scene below.

His mood was good—exceptionally good.

The wedding had gone superbly, achieving just what he'd wanted to achieve—his entry by marriage into the world that his bride took for granted as her birthright. A flicker of dark emotion moved in his mind—the bitter memory of being ejected from that Normandy chateau, unwanted and unwelcome, rejected and refused, reminding him that *he'd* had no such auspicious start.

His mouth tightened. Well, he did not need what his own mother had denied him! He had achieved it without her acceptance! Just as he'd made himself as rich as the father who'd repudiated him, denied any claim to paternity.

He shook the dark thoughts from him. They had no place in his life—not any longer. They had no more power to haunt him.

His gaze dropped to the woman at his side and his good mood streamed back. For three months— long, self-controlled months—he'd held himself on a tight leash. For three endless months he'd held himself back, knowing that above all the woman he had chosen for marriage was not a woman to be rushed. He must thaw the ice maiden carefully.

This moment now, as he leaned companionably beside her, was the reward for his patience. And soon he'd be reaping the full extent of that reward.

But not quite yet. Not until she was fully at ease with him, fully comfortable with him. The first few days of their honeymoon should achieve that. It would take more immense self-control on his part, this final stage of the process, but, oh, it would be worth it when she finally accepted his embraces. When she accepted the passion that would, he knew with masculine instinct, flare between them when the time was right.

He hauled his mind back to the present. For now it was still necessary for him to exercise patience. Self-denial.

He turned his head towards her with an easy smile, his voice casually amiable. 'What would you like to do for lunch?' he asked. 'We've flown east, so although you may feel as if it's only early morning, here the sun is high.'

She glanced at him, returning his easy smile, glad that it felt natural to do so. Glad that standing here beside him, side by side, seemed quite effortless. She could see how much more relaxed he was—just as she was. It might not be a honeymoon in the traditional sense, and he might have business affairs to conduct, but there was a holiday atmosphere all the same. She was enjoying the easy feeling it brought. Enjoying just being here.

'I don't mind,' she said. 'Whatever you prefer. And Nikos…' her voice changed slightly '…please don't feel you have to keep me company while we're here. I know you have business appointments and, really, in an ultra-luxurious hotel like this I'll be more than happy to lounge around lazily. And if I feel like anything more energetic I can always take a formal tour and go exploring. You know—souks and whatever. Even the desert, maybe. I'll be perfectly OK on my own, I promise.'

She said it quite deliberately, and was glad she had. She wanted to set the right tone, make it clear that she understood the unstated but implicit conditions of their marriage right from the off.

But he was looking at her strangely. Or so she thought. She gave an inner frown of puzzlement.

'Yes, I do have some business appointments,' he said, 'but I believe I can still find time for my bride on our honeymoon.' His voice was dry.

Her expression flickered, then recovered. 'Well, lunch together now would certainly be nice,' she said lightly. 'Do you think there's anywhere suitable to eat poolside? I must say, that water looks tempting.'

'Let's find out,' he returned. 'We'll take our swim-suits—be sure to apply enough sun cream. Your pale skin will burn instantly in these latitudes.'

They made their way down, bringing the cham-pagne bottle with them, and emerged into the hotel's vast atrium, in the centre of which an enormous crys-tal fountain cooled the already air-conditioned air and the fragrance of frankincense wafted all around.

She gazed openly at the opulence, and then Nikos was guiding her outdoors. The heat struck her again, and the sun's glare, and automatically she fished out her dark glasses from her tote bag. Nikos did likewise.

As she glanced at him she felt her tummy do a quick flip.

They'd both changed into casual gear—she into a floaty sun dress and he in chinos and an open-necked short-sleeved shirt—but somehow, from the moment he put on his sunglasses, there really was only one word to describe him.

Sexy.

It was such a cheap word—so redolent of dire TV

reality shows or girlish banter in the dorm. Not a word for a grown-up woman like her.

But it was the only word for him, and that was the problem. He just...*radiated* it. Whatever 'it' was. He had it in jaw-dropping amounts.

She tore her gaze away, grateful that her eyes were veiled with sunglasses too, berating herself silently for her illicit thoughts as they took their places at a shaded table in the open-air restaurant near the pools.

She gazed around in pleasure as Nikos recharged their champagne glasses. 'This really is gorgeous,' she said. 'Completely over the top, but gorgeous.'

He gave a laugh, taking the menu proffered by a waiter. He sounded relaxed, at ease. 'Well, be sure to mention that to the Prince when we meet him tomorrow.'

Diana stared. *'Prince?'* she echoed.

'Well, not the ruling Prince, but one of his nephews. He's the main driver behind development here—and I have an interest in various of his ventures—but he has to proceed carefully. Several of his cousins oppose him, and several more want to push for a Dubaistyle future. As it happens, we've been invited to his palace tomorrow for—of all things—afternoon tea.'

'Afternoon tea?' Diana echoed again.

'Yes, Sheikh Kamal's sister, Princess Fatima, is a big fan, apparently, and she welcomes any opportunity to partake of it.'

'Good heavens!' Diana exclaimed. 'Well, I dare say to an Arabian princess afternoon tea is as exotic as a desert banquet would be for me.' She frowned slightly. 'You'll have to guide me as to etiquette. I'm not at all *au fait* with royal protocol in the Middle East.'

'We'll get a briefing tomorrow morning from a palace official,' said Nikos. 'But I have every confidence in you, Diana.' He paused, then disposed of his dark glasses. His expression was serious. 'It's thanks to *you*, you know, that we've been invited to the palace. Were I here on my own I would only be receiving a brief audience on a strictly business basis, in his office. Whereas with you to accompany me it has become a social engagement and, as you are probably aware, that takes things to a completely different level in places like this. It will open doors for me.'

She met his gaze. 'I'm happy to be of use, Nikos. It makes me feel I'm…well, pulling my weight, I suppose.' Her tone altered as she inserted a lighter note. 'I'd better ensure I don't do anything to shock the Sheikh or his sister. '

'You'll be perfect,' he assured her. 'It comes naturally to you—knowing the correct way to behave in any social situation.'

She gave a self-deprecating moue. 'I can't claim any personal credit, Nikos. I've had a very privileged existence. It's people like *you*, you know, who didn't have those advantages and yet are where they are today by their own efforts and determination, who deserve credit. All of us are who we are completely by accident of birth—and none of us is responsible for that.'

Was there a sudden veiling of his eyes? A sense

of withdrawal behind a mask? If so, it made her conscious of just how little she knew about him. He had never spoken of his own background—only those few dismissive remarks about Greece. Other than that she'd gathered that he'd been brought up in France, spoke the language fluently, and he had made a passing reference to studying economics at one point.

As for his relationship with Nadya Serensky—she knew no more than what he had told her and that she did not have to feel any concern over his discarded trophy mistress. Nadya had married a Hollywood A-lister within weeks of Nikos finishing with her and was now queening it up in LA. Diana could not help but be relieved that she did not need to feel bad about helping herself to Nikos Tramontes.

For her own part, Diana had said very little about herself either. Nikos had asked no questions of her—and nor had she of him. After all, with their marriage being little more than a mutual business deal, there was no need for them to know anything much. All that was required was for them to be civil—friendly. Nothing more than that.

They enjoyed a leisurely lunch, and as it had during their engagement when they'd spent time together, Diana found the conversation flowing easily. Again, there was nothing personal in it—it was mostly about the Gulf, with Nikos briefing her as necessary to supplement what she already knew and then moving on to other parts of the world that her widely travelled husband was acquainted with.

It made for a perfectly pleasant meal, and after coffee they repaired to a poolside cabana. Diana changed in the private tented cubicle to the rear, emerging wearing a sleek turquoise one-piece and a cotton sarong in a deeper blue. The sarong revealed no more of her than her sundress had, and yet for all that she was aware of a sense of self-consciousness.

She sat herself down on a lounger, and was starting to anoint herself with sun cream when Nikos strolled up. He'd clearly changed elsewhere, and now dropped his bag on the lounger beside hers.

Diana tried hard not to stare—and failed dismally. *Oh, dear God...*

She'd known in her head that he must have a good physique—his wide shoulders, broad chest, and absolutely no sign of any flab on him anywhere was an indication of that. But there was a difference between knowing it and seeing it in the flesh.

Taut, muscled flesh was moulded like an athlete's, each pec and ab sculpted to perfection. She wished she'd jammed her concealing sunglasses back on her nose. Wished she could make her head drop. Wished she could just stop *staring* at him.

Her only saving mercy was that he didn't appear to notice her fixed gaze. Instead, he dropped down on his lounger and reached across in a leisurely fashion to help himself to one of the large selection of magazines that lay on a side table. Diana could see that it took him no effort at all to use simply his ab muscles to take the reaching weight of his body.

Urgently she pulled her gaze away, made a play of putting down her sun block.

Nikos settled back to read. His mood was even better than it had been before. He could see she'd also taken one of the magazines—not a glossy fashion one, he wouldn't have expected her to, but a popular history title. Satisfaction eased through him—and not just because he was very comfortably settled in a poolside cabana at an ultra-luxury hotel in the Gulf.

Because the woman he'd made his wife less than twenty-four hours ago was trying to pretend she was unaware of him right now.

He smiled inwardly. He'd been right to follow his instincts—to stick to his strategy of thawing the ice maiden Diana slowly before he moved in to melt her. He wanted her to relax in his company, lower her guard, become used to his constant presence.

So he gave no sign that he was perfectly aware of how aware she was of him, stripped to the waist, wearing only dark blue swim shorts, his long legs extended, feet bare. Instead he immersed himself in various articles in the financial magazine he'd helped himself to, while she read as well.

Their studied relaxation was only interrupted by intermittent enquiries from their personal butler as to whether they required anything.

He asked for mineral water, so did she, and then a glass of iced coffee, and both of them picked idly at a heaped plate of freshly cut fruit.

Eventually, with sun lowering and the heat of the day easing as the afternoon wore on, he tossed his reading aside.

'OK,' he announced, 'time for some exercise.' He

threw a smile at her and limbered to his feet. 'Fancy a dip?' he asked.

'I'd better, I think,' Diana agreed. 'Otherwise I'm going to snooze off…it's so restful here. And that will screw up my sleep patterns—jet lag's kicking in.'

He held out his hand and she took it, because to do otherwise would look pointed in a way she did not wish it to. He drew her up as though she weighed only a feather, and then loosed his grip as they walked towards the pool.

The sun, starting to lower behind the hotel to the west, shed a deep golden light over the water, which was shimmering in the heat. The main pool was relatively empty and Nikos strolled to the edge of the deep end, executing a perfect dive into the azure water, sending up a shower of diamond drops.

Diana couldn't help but watch him—watch the way his powerful, muscled body drove through the water, demolishing the length in seconds, only to double under in a tumble turn and head back towards her.

He surfaced, dark hair sleek around his face. 'Come on!' he instructed. 'It's warm as milk.'

To her relief, he didn't wait to watch her slip her sarong from her, and moments later she was in the water, dipping under the surface to get her head and hair wet. It was glorious—refreshing and cooling despite the ambient temperature of the pool.

She began a rhythmic traverse, contenting herself with breaststroke, enjoying the feeling of her long hair streaming behind her in the water, aware of Nikos steadily ploughing up and down only from the splashing of his arms in a strong, rapid freestyle. Having done the number of laps she was content with, she came to a halt at the far end and realised Nikos had also paused.

'Call it a day?' he asked. 'Shall we head back up and think about dinner?'

They got out of the water, put on the towelling gowns their butler had laid out for them, and headed back into the hotel. Diana was very conscious of her dripping hair, now wrapped in a turban. It would take a while to get ready.

It did, but Nikos left her to it, using the bathroom in the ancillary bedroom, obviously set aside for a child or a personal servant, leaving Diana in possession of the bridal bedroom and its palatial en suite bathroom. She was grateful for the unspoken tact with which Nikos had appropriated the other bedroom for himself.

By the time she emerged, over an hour later, she was ready for whatever demonstration of extreme opulence awaited her next. It proved to be an ultra-lavish bridal banquet, served to them in a private alcove off the main restaurant which was cantilevered out over the Persian Gulf.

The dress code, judging by the other diners, was formal, so she was glad she'd come prepared. Her silk gown, with its very fine plissé bodice, was in the palest eau-de-nil, and the soft folds of her long skirts brushed her legs as she walked in on Nikos's arm— an extended kind of body contact she was schooling herself to get used to now that she was his wife. With practice, she would soon lose her self-consciousness about it, she knew.

Her face lit up as they approached their table. 'Oh, how beautiful!' she could not help exclaiming.

Over the top it might be, but the table décor was exquisite. Huge bouquets of flowers flanked it on either side, and the floor was strewn with rose petals. More covered the table, which was also set with exquisite flowers, little candles, and napery constructed into swans—an image echoed on the side table, where stood an ice sculpture of two swans, their necks entwined in a heart shape, a feast of fresh sliced fruit and champagne chilling in a silver ice bucket.

With a low murmur of an appreciative 'Shukran!' to the bevy of waiting staff now ushering them into their chairs, she was aware that they were drawing the eyes of the other diners as they took their places.

Nikos had opted for the restaurant's speciality—a tasting menu. Tiny portions of exquisite and extraordinary concoctions that went on and on…and on.

'More?' Diana all but gave a mock groan as the waiting staff gathered to bestow upon them yet another tender trifle for their delectation.

'Keep going,' Nikos advised her, 'or the chef will be out here, brandishing his knives in rage at your lack of appreciation for his genius.'

She laughed, and got stuck in to yet another delicious morsel filled with flavours that were impossible to identify but which created a fantasy inside her mouth. She gave a murmur of intense appreciation and closed her eyes.

From across the table Nikos's gaze flickered over her. That little moan she'd given in her throat…that look of pleasure on her face…

He dragged his mind away. First their visit to the palace tomorrow, and then… Ah, *then* the honeymoon proper could begin. And how very much he was looking forward to that.

CHAPTER FIVE

'YOUR HIGHNESS.' DIANA dropped her head to the correct degree as she was formally presented to Sheikh Kamal and then his sister, Princess Fatima, who was at his side, also greeting their guests.

The Sheikh was, she had instantly appreciated, extremely handsome, with dark Arabian looks, a hawk-like nose, and piercing dark eyes from which, she suspected, little was hidden. But his manner to his guests was urbane in the extreme, and that of his sister fulsome.

Having been comprehensively briefed by one of the palace officials that morning in their hotel suite, Diana was confident she was not making any mistakes in protocol, and that her outfit of a long-sleeved, high-collared, ankle-length dress, worn with a loose but hair-concealing headscarf, was acceptable, and she found herself beginning to relax, encouraged by the warmth of their illustrious hosts' welcoming attitude.

'Afternoon tea' turned out to be an exact replica of what might be found in the UK, of the very highest standard, and she was not slow to say so. Her praise drew a giggle from Princess Fatima.

'My brother flew in the pastry chef from London this morning, and he brought all the ingredients with him to bake the scones just as you arrived!' Her dark eyes twinkled. 'Now, tell me,' she said confidentially, 'as an Englishwoman, what *is* the correct order in a cream tea? Jam first or clotted cream first?'

Diana gave a laugh. 'Oh, that's an impossible question, Your Highness. In Devon, I believe it is one way, and in Cornwall the other—but I never remember which! I'm afraid I do jam first.'

'So do *I*!' cried the Princess delightedly. She smiled warmly. 'I do hope, my dear, that we can take tea together when I am next in London?'

'I would be honoured and delighted,' Diana said immediately.

Nikos smiled. 'If it pleases the Princess,' he said, 'afternoon tea at Greymont would be our pleasure.'

Diana's fingers tightened on the handle of the priceless porcelain tea cup she was holding. A small but distinct sense of annoyance flared in her that Nikos had presumed to offer *her* home in his invitation to the sister of the man whose approval he needed to make money out of doing business here. Greymont was *hers*—and *she* would choose who to invite to it.

But he'd clearly said the right thing, and it obviously *did* please the Princess. Her eyes lit up. 'I *adore* English country houses,' she exclaimed in her enthusiastic manner.

'So much so that I bought my sister one only last year,' her brother interposed dryly.

'And so he did—he is the most generous of brothers,' Fatima acknowledged.

A chill replaced the flare of annoyance that Diana had been feeling.

If I hadn't married Nikos then Greymont might have been snapped up as the latest amusement for an Arabian princess.

It was a sobering reminder of just why she was sitting here, in a royal palace in the Persian Gulf, next to the man who was legally her husband, but in name only, making small talk with an Arabian princess about her latest acquisition.

The Princess rattled on in her bubbly manner, asking Diana about how great houses used to be run and how best to furnish them in a style to look authentic. Diana contributed as best she could, making several suggestions which the Princess seemed to value.

As she talked to the Princess, all the while taking delicate bites of the lavish cream tea laid before them, she became aware that the Sheikh and her new husband had moved their own conversation on to matters concerning the economic development of this particular Gulf state.

After a while, with the final sliver of Dundee fruit cake consumed, the final cup of Darjeeling taken, the Princess got to her feet.

'We shall leave the men to their tedious affairs,' she announced smilingly to Diana.

Nikos and the Sheikh immediately got to their feet as well, as did Diana, who was then swept off by the Princess. When they were in the Princess's own apartments Fatima cast aside her veiling, then turned to show Diana that she could do likewise with her headscarf.

'My dear, *what* a handsome husband you have.' She gave a theatrical sigh, her dark eyes gleaming wickedly. 'I'm going to tell my brother that he must lend you his...' She giggled even more wickedly. 'His *love-nest* in the desert. It's actually *quite* respectable— our great-grandfather had it built for his favourite wife, so they could escape together, away from his jealous older wives.'

'Oh, my goodness!' Diana exclaimed weakly, not knowing what to say.

'You must demand of your oh-so-handsome husband that he declares his love for you every morning. And even more importantly...' she cast a knowing look at Diana '...every *night*.'

Diana's expression was a study. It was impossible for her to comment, but fortunately for her the Princess took her silence as embarrassment.

'Oh, you English,' she cried laughingly. 'You are always so frozen—so...what is that word? Ah, yes—repressed. Well, I will not tease you—you are a bride. You are allowed to blush.' She took Diana's arm. 'Now, come and see my wardrobe. I am dying to show it to you.'

She led her off into a chamber which made Diana's

eyes widen. It was like, she realised, a museum of costume, for along the walls were a parade of gowns arrayed on mannequins set on pedestals, each and every one a priceless haute couture number, a work of art in its own right. Entranced, Diana let the Princess guide her around, enthusing volubly to the Princess's evident delight.

Then, to her dismay, the Princess exclaimed, '*This* one will be my wedding gift to you.'

She clapped her hands and one of her hovering servants hurried forward to receive instructions in rapid Arabic. Diana immediately demurred—a gown like this would cost thousands upon thousands. She couldn't possibly accept.

The Princess held up a hand, imperious now. 'To refuse it would be to offend,' she instructed regally.

Diana bowed her head. 'You do me too much honour, Highness,' she said formally, knowing she must concede.

'And *you* will do it justice,' the Princess returned warmly, adding for good measure 'The colour is all wrong for me. It makes my skin sallow. But you, with your fairness—ah, that shade of palest yellow is ideal.' She smiled. 'I will have it delivered.' The dark eyes gleamed with a wicked glint. 'Make sure you wear it at the *love-nest*.'

Again, Diana had no idea what to say—could only hope that the Princess would forget to speak to her brother about any such thing as a desert love-nest, which was the last place she wanted to go with Nikos. Meekly she let the Princess lead the way into another exquisitely decorated room, this time with a balcony overlooking a beautiful ornamental pool in a pillared courtyard.

'Tea,' the Princess announced, lowering herself onto a silk-covered divan and indicating that Diana should do likewise, 'but this time from *my* part of the world!'

The mint tea that was served proved very refreshing, and their conversation returned to the subject of historic English country houses. Diana waxed enthusiastic, mentioning the exhaustive restoration work she was having done on Greymont.

'You love your home dearly, do you not?' the Princess observed.

'It's the most important thing in the world to me!' Diana answered unguardedly.

The dark eyes rested on her curiously. 'Not your husband?'

Diana started, not sure what to say.

The Princess was still looking at her curiously. 'But surely you are in love with him more than anything in the world? If, after all, you had to choose between your home or your husband, surely there would be no choice at all?'

Diana swallowed. How could she answer?

Then, to her relief, a servant approached, bowing, then murmuring something to her hostess, who immediately got to her feet.

'We are summoned,' she announced.

A servant was there at once, with their headscarves, and once appropriately attired Diana followed the Princess from her private apartments back into the palace, to take her farewell of their hosts with Nikos.

As they settled back into the limousine that would return them to their hotel, she turned to him. 'How did it go? I hope the Sheikh was as gracious to you as his sister was to me.'

Nikos eased his shoulders back into the soft leather seat. 'Extremely well—just as I hoped after our having been invited socially,' he said with evident satisfaction. 'I have an agreement in principle from the Sheikh—which is essential—and clearance to talk to the relevant ministers. Exactly what I wanted.'

He looked at Diana and smiled warmly in a way that she must wish he hadn't.

'You did wonderfully. Thank you. I don't just mean all the protocol—I wouldn't insult you by implying you might not have been able to handle it—but the personal touch. The Princess clearly took to you… that was obvious—'

Diana cut across him, feeling flutteringly uncomfortable after that warm smile. 'Nikos, Princess Fatima has given me one of her couture gowns. It's worth a fortune, but she insisted. I know I couldn't refuse, but what on earth should I do now?'

'Make her a present of equal value,' he returned promptly. 'I don't mean financial—that would be crass, and anyway they have so much money it makes *me* look like a pauper, let alone you,' he said carelessly. 'I mean something matching.'

Diana furrowed her brow, and then a thought

struck her. 'I know! I'll find an antique gown for her—something she can possess but not wear because it's too historic. Maybe she can display it in her English country house when it's all done up.'

'Great idea,' said Nikos. He rested his eyes on her with warm approval, in that way she wished he wouldn't. 'You impressed the Sheikh, too, I could see that—he quoted from some Persian poet about how a beautiful and intelligent wife is the ultimate jewel a man can possess.' He paused, keeping that look on his face. 'And he was right about you being a jewel, Diana, both in beauty and intelligence. You are, indeed.'

For one long, endless second it seemed to her there was no breath in her body. Then, as if urgently grabbing a towel after emerging naked from the shower, she forced a little laugh to her lips.

'Well, I'm glad I came in useful this afternoon,' she said, and now her face was deliberately bright. 'And thank you for the opportunity to see inside a royal Arabian palace. It was like something out of a fairytale, and with a real-life prince and princess inside it too.'

Determinedly she went on to recollect with admiration some of the architectural details that had impressed her, even more determined *not* to mention anything about the Princess's talk about desert love-nests.

Hopefully Princess Fatima would forget all about it. A desert love nest was the last place that could be relevant to a marriage such as theirs.

A marriage in name only had no need of such a place.

* * *

'What do you say we dine up here tonight?'

Nikos's voice was casual as they walked into their huge suite and Diana's reply was immediate.

'Oh, yes, let's. I feel today has been quite a strain, and to be honest I could do with an evening just vegging.'

She rolled her head on her shoulders, rubbing at the nape of her neck.

'Need a massage?' Nikos gave a laugh and crossed towards her. He rested his hand on her neck and kneaded it gently with his fingertips.

It was a casual gesture, lasting only a few moments, but Diana froze. There was something about the weight of his large hand on her nape…something about the soft pressing of his fingers into her skin, the brush of his hand against the loosened tendrils of her hair caught into its habitual chignon…something that made her feel suddenly weak. Breathless.

'Better?' he murmured, and she realised that somehow he seemed to have stepped close to her, so that he stood just behind her. Close—so close.

Despite her frozen muscles, she seemed to be feeling a wash of intense relaxation easing through her—an impulse to roll her head forward and let free the low moan in her throat as she succumbed to the seductive touch of his fingers working at her neck.

Seductive?

With a scrambling of her senses she pulled herself together, made herself shake her head. *Seductive?* Was she mad to think such a thing?

She took a step away, freeing herself, and turned towards him with a bright smile. 'Lovely,' she said lightly. 'Thank you.'

She headed towards her bedroom. She needed a bit of sanctuary right now.

'I'm going to freshen up, then maybe order some fruit juice. The terrace looks very appealing at this time of day.'

Chattering brightly, she didn't look at him, just got inside her bedroom. She felt breathless. Determinedly, she inhaled. This had to stop. All this nonsense with her making such a fuss just because Nikos touched her. He hadn't meant anything by it—not a thing. And especially nothing *seductive*, for heaven's sake.

Yet a few minutes later, as she stood under the shower, warm water plunging like rainfall over her body, sluicing over her shoulders, her breasts, down over her flanks and legs, she felt a kind of restlessness inside her. An awareness of her own flesh and blood that was as rare as it was disturbing. As she smoothed the rich, foaming shower gel over herself, running her hands along her arms, her shoulders, her breasts and abdomen, there was a kind of sensuality about it...

As if it were not her own hands running over her body...

For one vivid, overpowering moment she had a vision of Nikos standing beside her in the steamy enclosure, the water sluicing over both of them as she stood in front of him, his strong arms enveloping her, his hands on her body, soothing, easing, smoothing...

caressing her as he washed her then turning her towards him, his arms sliding around her waist, drawing her to him...

She cut off the water. Furious with herself. What on *earth* was she thinking of? Nikos might be the man she'd married two days ago but he wasn't her husband in anything but name. It was totally out of order to think of him in any other way.

Determinedly she stepped out of the shower, towel-dried herself vigorously without the slightest hint of sensuality at all, deliberately not looking at herself in the glass as she did so, and got dressed as quickly as possible.

Friendliness—that was the only atmosphere she wanted between them, and that was what she was set on ensuring.

To her relief, that seemed to be Nikos's idea as well for the evening. So it was in an atmosphere of relaxed congeniality that they dined on their terrace, she wearing a simple cotton print dress with a thin lacy shawl around her shoulders, he in chinos and a polo shirt, feet in leather flip-flops, both of them casual and comfortable.

Unlike the elaborate tasting menu of the previous evening they chose more simple fare—grilled fish for herself, a steak for Nikos, followed by ice cream. Their conversation centred on chatting through the events of the afternoon, then Diana asked about his plans for the next day.

'If you're meeting those government ministers I'll either laze by the pool or go and browse in the souks.

Maybe both.' She smiled at Nikos, reaching for a piece of fruit to chase down the last of her wine.

He smiled at her in return, the lamp on the table softening his features. In the dim light, Nikos looked less formidable than he so often did.

'You're a very complaisant wife—do you know that, Diana?' he observed. 'How many other brides would be so undemanding?'

She gave a laugh. 'Good heavens, I'm perfectly capable of entertaining myself for a day, Nikos. So you go off and get your business done. Anyway, it's not like I'm a *real* bride, after all,' she finished lightly.

Was there a strange look in his eyes suddenly, or was it just the flickering candlelight?

His voice was lazily amused when he replied. 'That very swish wedding seemed real enough to me.'

She made a face. 'Oh, you know what I mean!' she exclaimed, taking another piece of fruit.

'Do I?' he replied, in that same lazily amused tone.

'Of *course* you do!' she said in mock exasperation.

She made herself look straight at him. She had to put it behind her—*right* behind her—that stupid, totally inappropriate mooning that had come over her when she'd been showering. There was no place for it—*none*, she told herself sternly.

I have to crush it down if it ever strikes again. Blank it and ignore it until it no longer exists.

He didn't answer, only continued to hold her gaze a moment longer with that same quizzical, amused look in his eye which she was making herself meet in a determinedly unaffected fashion. Then he broke contact, reaching for the bottle of wine and moving to refill her glass.

She covered it with her hand. 'I'd better not. I'm starting to yawn already,' she said.

She didn't want any more discussion about the nature of their marriage. It didn't need to be discussed. Let alone questioned. It was useful to both of them. Nothing more than useful. End of, she told herself firmly.

He accepted her decision. 'Well, it's been quite a day,' he said.

'It certainly has,' she said lightly.

Light—that's the way I have to be. Keeping everything nice and light. Or composed and businesslike. And friendly. Easy-going. Bright and cheerful. Or—

She ran out of adjectives that described the kind of behaviour that she needed to demonstrate for the next two years of marriage with Nikos.

A yawn started in her throat and she was unable to prevent it. She made another face. 'That's it, I'm calling it a day,' she said, and started to get to her feet. 'I'm off to bed.'

He stood up, helping her with her chair. He seemed very tall beside her suddenly.

'Goodnight, then,' he said. There was still that lazy note in his voice. 'Enjoy your bridal bed.'

There was nothing but amusement in his voice, Diana was sure, because obviously there couldn't be anything else. Not in a marriage like theirs.

So she answered in the same vein. 'Indeed I shall,'

she agreed. 'I wonder if it's been deluged in rose petals again?'

An eyebrow tilted. 'Shall I come and check for you?'

'Thank you, no. I'm sure I can sweep them away with my own fair hand,' she said, lightly but firmly.

Then she beat a retreat. Any banter, however light-hearted, about bridal beds and rose petals was best shut down swiftly. Any banter at *all* between her and Nikos about anything that could have the slightest sexual connotation should not even be acknowledged. It had no place in their marriage. None at all.

And she had to make sure it stayed that way. Absolutely sure.

The following day passed very pleasantly for Diana. Nikos went off to his business appointments and she went browsing in the tourist souks, lunched at the hotel, then had a lazy afternoon poolside.

Nikos returned early evening, just as she got back up to their suite, his mood excellent.

'Good meetings?' she enquired.

'Highly satisfactory,' he said.

He disappeared down to the pool to cool off, and by the time he came back up Diana was ready. They'd agreed to try out one of the other restaurants at the hotel, less formal than where they'd dined their first night. Tonight she wore a cocktail dress in pale blue had used minimum make-up and wore low-heeled shoes. Nikos looked relaxed and casual in an open-neck shirt, turned-back cuffs and no tie.

He looked devastatingly attractive, but she refused to pay attention to that fact. Instead she chattered on about her adventures in the souks as they tucked into the Italian-style dishes.

'Buy any gold?' he asked, with a lift of his eyebrow.

'A few bits and pieces,' she conceded. 'I know it's not hallmarked, but I couldn't resist. And,' she added, 'I bought a carpet! I saw it and thought it would be perfect for the library at Greymont—the one there is very moth-eaten now. I'm having it shipped home directly.' She made a moue. 'I probably got diddled over the price, because I'm not much good at haggling, but it seemed good value to me all the same. Cheaper than a dealer in London, at any rate.'

'A good morning's work,' he said, and smiled.

His mood was excellent, and not just because he'd had a very productive meeting with one of the Sheikh's key people, but also because Diana was clearly considerably more relaxed with him this evening. His careful strategy was working—get her comfortable with him, let her lower her guard, so she would be ready to accept what was inevitable between them. Ready to accept her own desire for him and his her for her.

The ice maiden melted in passion. Made mine at last...

And now, thanks to the Prince and Princess, he was going to be presented with the absolutely perfect setting in which to do so.

'Oh, desperately strenuous!' she laughed. 'So I rewarded myself with lazing by the pool all afternoon.'

He looked her over. 'You're starting to tan,' he said. 'It suits you.'

There was nothing particularly provocative in the way he was inspecting her, but she had to steel herself all the same.

'How sweet of you to notice,' she said, making her voice lightly humorous. 'I'm still using huge amounts of sun cream all the same!'

He smiled. 'Well, make sure you take plenty with you when we head off into the desert tomorrow.'

She looked at him. 'Desert?' Had he planned an expedition? Dune-bashing perhaps?

But it was not dune-bashing.

'Yes. I've had a communiqué from the palace.' He paused, letting his eyes rest on Diana. 'Apparently it has pleased the Princess to request that her brother the Sheikh lends us the use of his…ah…"desert love-nest", I believe is the term the Princess used, since we are here on our honeymoon…'

Dismay filled Diana's face. 'Nikos, we can't *possibly* accept!'

She'd deliberately not told him what Princess Fatima had said to her—had hoped the Princess would forget all about it, or that her brother would turn down any request she might make. But in vain…

His expression changed. 'Diana, we can't possibly *not*.' His tone was adamant. 'It would cause grave offence to do so. It's a singular honour, and an indication of how the Princess has taken to you.'

'To refuse would be to offend…' Diana echoed in a hollow voice.

'Exactly,' Nikos confirmed in that same steely voice. Then his expression softened, and there was a humorous glint in his eye now. 'Think of it as an adventure. You'll be able to dine out on it in years to come.'

She gave a disheartened sigh. 'I suppose so,' she said reluctantly.

Her mood had plummeted. For a start, she felt a total hypocrite. A complete fraud. Here was Princess Fatima, bestowing upon her what she fondly imagined would be a fantastically romantic interlude, when it was the very last thing that was appropriate for her and Nikos.

But there was more to her dismay than the consciousness of being a hypocritical fraud. The thought of being wafted off to a desert hideaway, all on her own with Nikos...

Sternly, she rallied herself. There was nothing she could do to evade this, and it would, after all, be very good schooling for her to get more and more used to being with Nikos. It would help her to get over this ridiculous overreaction to him she had.

It was an instruction she kept repeating to herself as they set off the next day, heading out into the desert in a luxurious leather-seated, air-conditioned SUV with jacked-up wheels that would clear the desert sand, shielded from the burning heat outside.

It was a heat that deepened as they left the coast and drove along black metalled roads that glistened in the sunshine, first across scrubby flat land and then snaking amongst towering sand dunes that signalled the start of the fabled Empty Quarter.

Diana gazed rapt at the desert scenery which was gradually becoming rockier. The road wound through deep gullies and past oases of palm trees, with few signs of habitation and an occasional glint of murky-looking water. Camels—some being herded along in a chain, some merely wandering on their own, presumably either wild or having been let out to graze as and where they could—wandered along the roadside sometimes, but otherwise there was little visible sign of life.

Though they'd set out early in the morning, in order to catch what amounted to the coolest part of the day, it was nearing lunchtime when they finally arrived. They had been through a village of sorts, and what looked to Diana's eyes like some kind of military base, and now, about half an hour's drive thereafter, a building hove into view that at first she thought merely to be an outcrop of rock.

But she realised as they approached that it was a small, square building, made of the same sand-coloured stone as the earth, two storeys tall against the surrounding desert. Only a perimeter fence indicated that there was something special about the place—and the guards standing to attention as they drove through the metal gates to approach the building itself. High, arched double doors opened wide, and the four-by-four drove through with a flourish to enter what was soon revealed to be an outer courtyard.

Along with Nikos she climbed down. Palace servants were running forward to help. At once the heat struck her, clamping around her like a vice. Immediately she felt perspiration bead on her spine, despite the loose cotton shirt she was wearing. The glare of the sun after the tinted windows of the vehicle made her reach for her dark glasses.

'We need to get inside,' Nikos murmured, putting his arm around her waist and guiding her forward.

She craned her head as she walked towards the ornately carved inner doors that were opening as if controlled by a magic genie, and entered what she realised was the inner courtyard—the palace itself.

The love-nest.

CHAPTER SIX

DIANA GAVE A gasp of pleasure.

'Oh, how absolutely beautiful!' she exclaimed spontaneously.

The courtyard was an exquisite garden—an oasis with trickling fountains in stone basins, little channels that wound about bordered by greenery, the whole edged with vine-covered columns creating shady arbours under which marble benches were set.

They were ushered forward by bowing servants into the interior of the bijou palace, and Diana gazed in pleasure at the delicate fretwork archways and the inlaid marble columns as they went up to the upper floor where the royal apartments were. There might be only one bedroom, huge though it was, but the day room—or whatever it might be called in Arabic—contained plenty of silk-swathed divans, which would, she hoped uneasily, solve the sleeping situation.

Quite how she would cope she didn't know, but somehow she would. She must.

For now, though, what she wanted was a bathroom to freshen up in, and she was relieved to discover it was western in style. Even so, as she took a cooling shower she kept her water usage to the minimum, mindful that they were in the middle of a desert. Then she donned a calf-length, floaty, fine cotton flower-printed dress, draped a chiffon scarf over her hair and bare shoulders.

She found Nikos, also showered and changed, waiting for her by an arched colonnade that looked out on the wide room-length balcony. Lunch had been set out for them, and as they took their places, soft-footed servants unobtrusively waiting on them, Diana resolved that however inappropriate being in an Arabian love-nest might be for her and Nikos, they might as well make the most of this privileged stay.

Lunch passed congenially while they chatted in what had now become quite a comfortable fashion, on subjects roaming from the journey they'd had that morning to more intellectual consideration of the geo-politics of the region and the impact on world affairs and global economics.

Nikos was, as Diana already knew, very well in-formed, and she found it stimulating to discuss such matters with him. It struck her that he was a far more interesting person to talk to than most of her friends and acquaintances. He had a world view that they lacked, a broadness of opinion and a highly incisive intelligence. No wonder he'd come so far in his life.

I never find his company tedious, she found her-self thinking.

So often when she was talking to people socially she was conscious of simply going through the motions—

saying what was proper, most of it trivial but socially acceptable, anodyne, appropriate to the occasion. She could do it in her sleep, but it was hardly a mental workout. Exchanging views and arguments with Nikos was quite the opposite, and she found that she really enjoyed trying to keep up with him.

We get on surprisingly well.

The thought was suddenly in her head, lingering a moment, and then, as the leisurely meal ended, Nikos brought the subject round to themselves again.

'So, how do you want to spend the afternoon?' he asked her. His tone was easy, relaxed, his glance at her the same.

'Camel riding?' she suggested, with a hint of humour in her voice.

He nodded. 'We must most definitely do so while we are here—but not in the main heat of the day. However, there's a pool if we want it—though for me...' Nikos flexed his long legs '...I wouldn't mind a good workout after our long drive and this highly delicious lunch—there's a gym here too.'

'Well, why don't you?' Diana smiled amiably, then smothered a yawn. 'I have to say that our early-morning start and that large lunch is making taking a siesta very tempting!'

And that was what she did, dozing peacefully for a good couple of hours or more.

The palace had been built long before air-conditioning, and used the ancient Arabian technique of maximising the up-draught of air through cleverly positioned open archways and slatted wooden windows to create a cooling effect.

When she finally arose, much refreshed, it was to be served with mint tea and tiny pastries, before going to change into her swimming costume and sarong and being shown down to the pool. It was situated in the gardens that stretched beyond the palace, away from the entrance they'd arrived at, bordered by a high stone wall and fronted by palm trees for total privacy.

The heat was beginning to ebb, she fancied, and once she was wet it was much cooler as she swam lazily around, feeling her loose hair streaming sleekly behind her. A sense of well-being eased through her. This really was a magical experience, and however inapplicable it was for her and Nikos to be here in the Sheikh's love-nest it was not an experience she would ever have again.

'So this is where you are.'

Nikos's voice penetrated her consciousness and she looked up from her lazy circling of the pool to see him standing at the water's edge. He looked even taller from this low perspective, and he'd clearly done a vigorous workout indeed. His T-shirt was damp, so were his shorts, and his muscles were pumped.

A moment later she saw even more than his shoulders, biceps and quads. He peeled off the damp shirt and chucked it, then yanked off his trainers. A moment later he was in the pool beside her, under the water, then surfacing in a flurry of diamond droplets, shaking the water from his eyelashes and grinning.

'Wow! That feels good!' he exclaimed feelingly. He looked at Diana. 'Apparently the temperature will start dropping once the sun has set, and for that I shall be grateful.' He quirked an eyebrow in his characteristic manner. 'Do you fancy some star-gazing later on? There's a very fancy telescope up on the roof, I'm told, but even without that the show should be spectacular.'

As he spoke, he found himself thinking about Nadya for a moment. He'd never have made such a suggestion to *her*. She'd have looked at him as if he were mad, and then counter-suggested going to a fashionable nightspot instead, where she could enjoy being seen and admired.

He frowned inwardly. Had he really never noticed how limited Nadya was? She was a professional to the hilt in her work, but when it came to anything else—from astronomy to geopolitics—her eyes would glaze over.

Diana's eyes brightened and sharpened—she listened and responded, sometimes agreeing, sometimes arguing a counterpoint, putting a different perspective and engaging vigorously, holding her corner, but open to new views as well.

She was open to the prospect of studying the night sky too. She was smiling enthusiastically at his suggestion, as he'd thought she would.

'Oh, yes please!' she said eagerly.

'Great,' Nikos returned, banishing the memories of Nadya's time in his life, utterly irrelevant to him now that he had Diana.

Diana, who was opening the door to the next stage of his life with her impeccable background, her very own stately home, the upper-class world she had been born into and which he would now enjoy as her husband, the world she took for granted, the world he himself had had no right to. Diana would give him that and more.

Diana was the woman he desired for her cool pale beauty, the woman he was so close to making his own in the most intimate way.

Soon...so very soon now.

With a flexing of his muscles he executed a perfect duck-dive and disappeared under the water completely, swimming strongly to the end of the pool and back several times before needing to surface.

Diana watched him admiringly. 'That's amazing breath control,' she told him as he finally broke the water.

He grinned again. 'It's just practice,' he said. 'And good lung capacity.'

Diana's eyes went to the smooth, muscled expanse of his chest, with its perfectly honed pecs and taut solar plexus in the flat between his hard-edged ribs. She looked away hurriedly. Feasting her gaze on his near naked body was no way to behave.

She waded to the steps and clambered out, wrapping a towel around herself. 'I'm heading indoors,' she announced. 'Time to shower. What's the drill for this evening?' Her voice held the light, bright tone she was determined to keep with him.

'Sunset drinks on the terrace,' he informed her. 'No rush.'

It was just as well he'd said that, Diana discovered, for when she returned indoors she was immediately swept away by what seemed to be a whole posse of waiting women who, with a flurry of soft-footed, smiling attention, proceeded to get her ready for the evening.

For a brief moment she resisted—then relented. After all, never again would she be staying in a royal hideaway in the Arabian desert—so why not indulge in what was being so insistently offered to her?

With murmurs of *'Shukran!'* she gave herself up to their ministrations.

Nikos stood on the wide upper-storey terrace, edged by a balustrade in the red sandstone that the whole building was constructed with, smooth and warm to the touch still, though the sun was close to setting. To the east, colour was fading from the sky, and soon stars would be pricking out in the cloudless sky. There would indeed be a spectacular show later on.

Ruminatively he sipped his drink, a cool, mint-flavoured concoction that went well with the ambience. There was champagne on ice awaiting Diana's eventual emergence. His eyes narrowed slightly as he recalled that moment in the pool, when she'd made no secret of being oh-so-aware of his body. Finding it pleasing to her.

Anticipation thrummed softly through him. Finally...*finally* he was losing the ice maiden! It had taken him this long, but the thaw was underway. He felt the tug of a caustic smile at the corner of his mouth as his eyes rested on the desert vista beyond. In this heat, how could she help but thaw?

And here, now, in this the ultimate hideaway, she would melt completely, he knew.

Mentally he sent a message of thanks to the Sheikh and his romantic-souled sister. This place was absolutely ideal. The hotel might have been designed to convey the impression of *Arabian Nights*—but this was the real thing.

His smile lost its caustic edge and widened into one of true appreciation. An appreciation he knew Diana shared too. There was an authenticity to this place that appealed to her—it had a history, a cultural heritage. Generations had passed through it, leaving the echo of their presence, and that made it similar in essence to her own country house home. He felt it was a good omen for their stay.

A sound behind him made him turn. And as he did every thought about the edifice he was in vanished. Every thought in his head vanished except one.

It was Diana—and she looked...

Sensational.

She was walking towards him slowly. Slowly, he realised, because she was in very high heels and her dress was very tight. It must, he realised instantly, be the couture gown gifted to her by the Princess. And, oh, the Princess had chosen well!

The superbly crafted gown contoured Diana's figure like a glove, fitting her almost like a second skin.

There was nothing at all immodest in the fit—it simply skimmed over her flawlessly, the smooth, pale yellow material creating a sheen that glistened in the fading light, aglow from the setting sun reflecting off the golden dunes.

He gazed at her, riveted, as she approached, the short train of the dress swishing on the marble floor, the delicate beading rustling at her bodice and hem.

She stopped as she came up to him. 'The Princess had this delivered here!' she announced.

She'd been half dismayed to discover that Princess Fatima had kept to what she'd promised, and half dazzled by wearing so exquisite a gown, far in excess of what her own wardrobe ran to.

Nikos's eyes swept over her. 'You look fantastic,' he breathed.

His whole body had tensed, tautened, and he could not take his eyes from her. The incredible gown— haute couture at its most extravagant best—needed no jewellery. The beading served as that, and all that had been added was a kind of narrow bandeau of the same material, embroidered all over with the delicate beading that had been woven through the elaborate coiffure of her hair. Her make-up was subdued, but absolutely perfect for her, her lips a soft sheen, her skin unpowdered, her eyelashes merely enhanced, and a little kohl around the eyes themselves. It made her look sensual and exotic.

'It's incredible,' he murmured, still sweeping his gaze over her. He found himself reaching for her hands—their nails were pearlescent, with a soft sheen like her lips. Slowly he raised them to his mouth. His eyes met hers. 'You were always beautiful,' he said, 'but tonight—tonight you surpass the stars themselves!'

For a moment their eyes met and mingled. Held. Something seemed to pass between them...something that she could not block—did not wish to. Something that seemed to keep her absolutely motionless while Nikos beheld her beauty.

Then, with a little demur, she slipped her hands away and gave a tiny shake of her head. 'It's the gown,' she said. 'It's a work of art in its own right.'

'Then it needs a toast of its own!' Nikos laughed.

A servant was hovering, waiting to open the champagne, and Nikos nodded his assent. A moment later he was handing Diana a softly beaded flute and raising his own.

'To your gown—to its exquisite beauty.' He paused. A smile lurked at his mouth, and his eyes were not on the gown. They were on Diana. 'And to you, Diana, my most exquisitely beautiful bride.'

She gazed up at him, her own glass motionless, and met his dark, lustrous eyes, so warm, so speaking...

And suddenly out of nowhere, out of the soft desert night that was slowly sweeping towards them from the east, as the burning sun sank down amongst the golden dunes, she felt a sense of helplessness take her over. She hadn't wanted to come to this place—this jewel-like desert hideaway, this royal love-nest dedicated to sensual love—but she was here. Here and now—with this man who, alone of all the men she had ever encountered, seemed to have the ability to make her shimmer with awareness of his overpowering masculinity.

She simply could not bring herself to remember that he was the man who was saving Greymont for her, to whom she was to be only a society wife, playing the role that he wanted her to play at his side.

How could she think of things like new roofs for Greymont and rewiring, restoring stonework and all the bills that came with that? How could she think of being just a useful means for Nikos Tramontes to move in circles he had not been born into? And how could she think of things like marriages of convenience that were nothing more than business deals?

It was impossible to think of such things! Not standing here, in this priceless precious gown, with a glass of vintage champagne between her fingers as she stood looking out over the darkening desert, miles and miles from anywhere, alone with Nikos.

So she raised her glass to him, took a first sip, savouring the delicate *mousse* of the champagne.

'To you, Nikos,' she said softly. 'Because I would not be here were it not for you.' Her eyes held his still. 'And, as you say, this is an experience of a lifetime…'

Something changed in his eyes—a fleck of gold like flame, deep within. 'It is indeed, my most beautiful bride.'

A frisson went through her and she was powerless to stop it. Powerless to do anything but look back at him and smile. Drink him in. Her eyes swept over him. He was wearing narrow-cut evening trousers, but not a dinner jacket. His dress shirt, made of silk, was tieless, open at the neck, his cuffs turned back and fastened with gold links that caught the last of the setting sun and exposed his strong wrists.

He looked cool, elegant and—she gulped silently—devastatingly attractive. His freshly shaved jawline, the sable hair feathering at his nape and brow, the strong planes of his features and those dark, deep-set, inky-lashed eyes that were meeting her gaze, unreadable and yet with a message in them that she could not deny.

Did not wish to deny…

Emotion fluttered in her again. How far away she was from the reality of her life—how immersed she was, here, in this fairytale place, so remote, so private, so utterly different from anything she had known.

It's just me and Nikos—just the two of us.

The real world seemed very far away.

She felt a quiver in her blood, her pulse, felt sudden breathlessness. Something was happening to her and she did not know what.

Except that she did…

She took another mouthful of the rare-vintage champagne, feeling the rush of effervescence in the costly liquid create an answering rush in herself. She felt as light as air suddenly, breathless.

She became aware that the silent-footed servants were there again, placing tempting delicacies on golden platters on an inlaid table, bowing and then seeming to disappear as noiselessly as they had appeared.

'How do they do that?' Diana murmured as she leant forward to pick at the delicate slivers of what, she did not know—knew only that they tasted delicious and melted in her mouth like fairy food.

'I suspect a magic lamp may be involved,' Nikos answered dryly, and Diana laughed. Then he smiled again—a smile that was only for her—and met her eyes. He raised his glass again. 'To an extraordinary experience,' he said, his slight nod indicating their surroundings.

She raised her own glass and then turned her attention to the darkening desert. 'I shall certainly remember this all my life,' she agreed. Her gaze swept on upwards. 'Oh, look—stars!'

'There'll be a whole lot more later on,' Nikos said. 'For now, let's just watch the night arrive.'

She moved beside him, careful not to lean on the balustrade lest the work of art she was wearing was marked or creased in any way. Her mood was strange.

She had given herself over to the murmuring attentions of what she could only refer to as handmaidens, letting them do what they willed with her. It had started with them bathing her, in water perfumed with aromatic oils, and gone on from there until she'd walked out on to the terrace feeling almost as if she were in a dream.

Because surely it *must* be a dream—standing here beside Nikos, watching the night darken over the dunes, hearing the strange, alien noises of night creatures waking and walking, feeling the air start to cool, the air pressure change. How far away from the real world they seemed. How far away from everything that was familiar. How far away from everything that was not herself and Nikos.

Her eyes went to him again, seeing his elegantly rakish garb, the absence of a tie, the open-necked shirt, the turned-back cuffs, all creating that raffish look, looking so *sensual*.

She felt a ripple of ultra-awareness go through her like a frisson. As if every nerve-ending were suddenly totally alert—quivering. And as she stood beside him she caught his scent—something musky, sweet-spiced and aromatic, that went perfectly with this desert landscape, matching the oh-so-feminine version of the perfume with which she had been adorned. It caught her senses, increasing the tension that was vibrating silently through her as she stood beside him, so aware of his presence close to her, knowing she only had to lean a little sideways for her arm to press against his. For his arm to wrap around her, pull her to him as they stood gazing out over the darkening desert.

From somewhere deep within her another emotion woke. One she should pay heed to. One that called to her to listen. But she would not listen. She refused to listen. Refused to heed it. She would only go on standing here, nestled into the strong, protective curve of Nikos's arm, gazing out over the desert that surrounded them all about, keeping the world beyond far, far away.

She sipped her champagne, as did he, and they stood in silence until the night had wrapped them completely and the dunes had become looming, massy shapes, darker than the night itself. Overhead, stars had started to blaze like windows into a fiery furnace beyond. Behind them torches were being lit by unseen hands along the length of the terrace, and several braziers, too, to guard against the growing chill of the desert night, and the flickering firelight danced in the shadows all around them.

She turned, and realised that through the archways that pierced the inner border of the terrace more light was spilling—softer light—and the characteristic sweetly aromatic scent of Middle Eastern cuisine.

'Ready to dine?' Nikos asked her with a smile, and she nodded, suddenly hungry.

Lunch seemed a long time ago. Her everyday reality a long time ago.

Because this surely wasn't real, was it? Nikos as her very own desert prince, dark-haired, dark-eyed, and she, gliding beside him like a princess, in a gown fit for royalty, her train swishing on the inlaid marble floor.

Servants were guiding them forward, smiling and bowing, ushering them into yet another room. She gave a soft cry of delight as they entered. It was a dining room, the interior constructed out of wood, fretted and inset with tessellations which glinted in the light of the dozens of candles that were the only illumination, burning in sconces on the walls and pillars all around, and on the table set for them with golden dishes, golden plates—golden everything, it seemed.

The air was heavy with the fragrance of frankincense from hidden burners.

'*Jamil jaddaan*—very beautiful!' Diana exclaimed, clapping her hands in delight and indicating the exquisite room.

The servants bowed and smiled, and the steward pulled back huge carved wooden chairs, lined with silk cushions, for her and Nikos. She took her place carefully, and Nikos sat opposite her.

The meal that followed was as exquisite as the room they dined in—dishes of rich, fragrant Middle Eastern food, with delicately spiced charcoal-baked meats as familiar as lamb and as unfamiliar as goat and camel, and who knew what else besides, as tender as velvet, all served with rice enhanced with nuts and dates and raisins, sweet and savoury at the same time.

As a mindful precaution for her priceless gown Diana had called for a shawl to be brought, which she'd swathed around her upper body while she ate.

'I couldn't bear to mark this dress!' She shuddered at the thought. 'I doubt it could ever be cleaned—and even if it could the cost would be terrifying!' She looked at it musingly. 'I wonder when I'm ever going to have an opportunity to wear it again.'

He answered instantly. 'When we entertain at Greymont,' he said. 'Once all the work is complete we can give a grand ball—and you shall wear the Princess's gown for it.'

A vision leapt in her mind instantly. Greymont, thronged with guests, and she and Nikos descending the stairs to the hall, her hand on his arm—man and wife, side by side. As if their marriage was a true one.

For a moment longing fired within her. So fierce she felt faint with it.

What if my marriage to Nikos were real?

The thought wound its way around her senses, enticing, beguiling, sweet and fragrant—just as the fragrance of the frankincense was winding its way around her senses, along with the glowing effervescence of champagne, the deep, rich sensuality of the wine, her physical repletion after the delicately spiced foods, the soft golden light of the candles, reflected a million times in the golden dishes...

The light was setting off the man she had married a few short days ago with a golden sheen, softening the contours of his face, giving him glints like flecks of gold in his dark, long-lashed eyes.

Eyes that were resting on her.

With a message in them that was as old as time.

'Diana.'

He said her name in a low voice, setting down his wine glass slowly, paying it no attention. All his focus was on her, now, as she sat there, held in his gaze.

'Diana...'

He said her name again. His voice was husky now. How beautiful she was! Like a rare, exquisite jewel, shining in this jewel box of a room. For him alone.

He got to his feet, oblivious of the servant who was instantly there, drawing back the heavy, carved cedarwood chair. He held out a hand towards Diana. Slowly, very slowly, she got to her feet. Unnoticed, her swathing shawl fell to the floor. Unnoticed, a servant stooped to pick it up, drape it gracefully around her shoulders.

Wordlessly she took Nikos's hand. It closed over hers, warm and strong. She felt faint suddenly, and filled with a subliminal sense of anticipation. His eyes smiled at her—warm, like his handclasp.

'Shall we look at the stars?' he said softly.

Still wordless, she nodded. There was a breathlessness in her—a headiness that had nothing to do with the consumption of champagne and wine and everything to do with Nikos holding her hand, leading her away.

They went back out on to the wide marble terrace and down to the far end where, Diana realised, there was a flight of steps that would take them upwards to the roof.

As they gained the flat surface she gave an audible gasp. Only a very dim torch, low down, lit the top of the steps. Beyond there was velvet darkness. A darkness that was pierced only above their heads by a forest of stars, the incandescence of them burning through the floor of heaven.

She lifted her hand. 'It's as if I could reach up and pluck one down, they seem so close!' she said in wonder.

Nikos tucked her hand into the crook of his arm, leading her carefully, mindful of her high heels, into the centre of the wide flat rooftop, which was carpeted like a roofless open-air room. Roofed by stars.

The sky was like a bowl, inset with stars down to

the horizon, or so it seemed—a horizon marked only by the rounded edges of the dunes, the jagged out-lines of rocks and outcrops. She gazed about her, lips parted, awestruck, tilting back her head.

She dimly was aware that she was leaning against the strong column of Nikos's body to give herself bal-ance. He was gazing upwards too, his gaze sweeping in wide arcs to take it all in. He started to name the constellations that were visible at these latitudes, at this season, raising his arm to guide her.

'It's the most glorious thing I've seen in my life!' She sighed, still breathless with awe.

'Do you want the telescope set up?' he asked her, but she shook her head.

'No, for tonight this is enough—I can't take it all in as it is.' She turned to face him. 'Oh, Nikos, this is the most wonderful sight!'

'It is indeed,' he said. 'And we can see them bet-ter still if we lie down…'

He gestured to something that had not at first been visible to Diana, but now, with her darkness-adjusted eyes, she saw that—incongruous as it might appear—there was what seemed to be a king-sized divan in the centre of the rooftop, presumably set there for the very purpose of lying down to see the stars. Already her neck was aching with tilting her head upwards, and her feet in their high heels were scarcely prepared for long standing.

Gratefully she let Nikos guide her, help her to ease down, to take off her shoes—not needed now—and then lie back on the myriad cushions piled on the silk-covered divan.

'Oh, that's better,' she said gratefully, able now to gaze straight up at the night sky.

She felt the divan dip slightly as Nikos's heavy form came down on the other side. With half her mind she felt a flicker go through her—maybe she and Nikos lying virtually side by side like this, all alone under the desert night sky, was not the wisest thing. Then she brushed it aside. This was an experience to be made the very most of. They were here to star-gaze—nothing else.

For a while they simply lay quietly, gazing upwards. Speech seemed not just superfluous, but intrusive. The cushion beneath Diana's head was soft, but because of her elaborate coiffure it was not entirely comfortable. She shifted position slightly, and then heard Nikos speak beside her in the dark.

'What is it?'

'It's my hair,' she said. 'This style is designed to be vertical, not horizontal.' She propped herself up, reaching with her other hand behind her head, patting it to see where the pins were.

'Let me help,' said Nikos.

He levered himself to a sitting position and turned her shoulders slightly, to give him greater access to the back of her head. For reasons she did not want to explore, Diana let him. It was easier for him to do it than for her.

But there was more about this than ease of access. She dipped her head slightly. And as his fingers worked gently over the intricate plaits and coils, seeking pins and grips, she felt a great sensuous languor creep over her. His touch was delicate, feathering through her hair, and as each pin was removed she felt its loosening go through her. Felt a slow surge of blood start to pulse through her.

'Oh, that feels so good…' She sighed as coil after coil was released, easing the tension on her skull. She felt her locks cascading loose to her shoulders, nothing restraining them at all but the beaded bandeau threaded through them.

'Does it?' said Nikos softly.

Her hair was loose now, all the pins and grips discarded—presumably, she thought absently, on the carpet surrounding the divan. But the thought was vague, inchoate. Irrelevant in comparison with that oh-so-sinuous languor that was stealing over her.

Nikos's fingers were still threading through her hair, softly smoothing her locks, gently kneading her scalp, just above her nape. Instinctively she dipped her head further, giving a little sigh of pleasure. She heard his low laugh again, felt his sensuously working fingertips move to the tops of her ears. Then, with another silvered quickening of her pulse, she felt his thumb idly tease at a lobe. A million quivers of sensation went through her. It felt *so* good…

There was a haze inside her, around her. Above, the stars were blazing in their glory, but she felt her eyelids dip, made a little sound in her throat.

As she did so, she felt Nikos's hand stroke down her throat, its slender column caressed by his long, sensitive fingers. She felt her face being turned towards him, felt her eyelids fluttering open—to see him looking down at her.

And in his eyes, in the starlight, was what she could not deny.

Did not want to deny.

She said his name. Just his name. Breathed it like a sigh.

Who was there to hear it but him and the empty desert? The desert and the night. The night and the stars. The stars and Nikos.

Nikos—who, alone of all the men in all the world, seemed to possess what no man had ever possessed before.

The power to enthral her. Entice her. Tempt her. Tempt her to do what she was doing now—what she *must* do, it seemed, here, now, on this soft silken divan under the burning desert stars, where nothing else existed but themselves and the night and their desire. His for her, hers for him.

I want him so much... So much...

She did not know why—did not care—only knew that her hand was lifting to feather at his temple, to graze the sable hair and drift down the planed cheek to edge along the roughened outline of his jaw.

Her eyes were still half closed, her body still filled with that incredible heaviness. And as she touched him she made that little sound in her throat again, felt as if in a dream that her breasts were tightening, quickening under the second skin that was her precious, priceless gown. The gown given to her by a princess—a princess who'd asked for this desert love-nest to be theirs. For now. For tonight.

It wasn't what their marriage was about—she knew that—but she couldn't think of it now. Could only think and feel what was happening to her here, beneath the desert night burning with myriad stars.

Yearning filled her, and an instinct so powerful she could not resist it. She had no wish to resist it—not here, not now, not under these burning desert stars, not under the heavy-lidded gaze of the man whose mouth was now lowering slowly, infinitely slowly, to meet hers.

His kiss was like silken velvet—infinitely soft, infinitely sensuous. Infinitely arousing. That little sound came from her again, deep in her throat. She felt her neck arch, her loosened wanton hair sliding like satin, felt the hot pulse at her throat strengthen. She felt her hand slip around the nape of his neck, draw him down to her as she rested slowly back-wards, moving down upon the waiting cushions, her hair now spilling out across them.

He came down with her, his kiss starting to deepen. She felt her breasts cresting, straining against the bod-ice of her gown, and still he kissed her as if he would never release her. Desire was sweeping up inside her. A desire whose power she had never known, had only glimpsed in brief glances, crushed thoughts, when-ever she'd looked at the man she had married—who was not hers to glance at like that, not hers to think about, not hers to desire…

Except for this night.

She could have him for this night only! Here, where the rest of the world had ceased to exist, seemed as if it might never exist again, might never have existed at all. For only the stars were burning in their own eternity. An eternity she could share for this one night only…

Nikos—the only man to arouse her, awaken her. The only man to whom she was a woman—a woman who could feel what other women felt.

Never… Never have I felt this desire before! Never!

But now she did—now she knew its power, its force and strength. It was arousing and inspiring her, sweeping her along with its tide so that she could not resist, taking her to a new land—a land she had thought was not for her, had never found before.

But she had found now…with him…with Nikos.

The land of sweet desire.

Desire that was mounting in her now, quickening in her blood, in her heating body, in her shallow, hectic breath. She felt her fingers mould his nape, spear into his hair, felt her body turn towards him like a magnet.

Bliss was seeping up inside her at the drowning sweetness of feeling his lips grazing hers—lips that were slowly, remorselessly, teasing from her a deeper response now, a response that began a restlessness inside her, a sense of going over the edge, giving up all control. Giving it up to the feelings filling her body, her mind, her very being.

Of their own volition, in their own mounting need, her lips parted and she gave that low moan in her throat again—of relief, of pleasure, of wonder and bliss as she tasted to the full all that Nikos was offering, all that he was doing, giving to her, with a touch so skilled, so arousing, that she was blind with it.

He was murmuring her name even as he kissed her, tasted her, his hand slipping down, sliding slowly and sensually over the bodice of the dress to mould the contours of her body. Her spine arched into his caress. She was aching for his hand to close over the straining mound of her breast, and when it did, his palm grazing the straining crests, she felt another surge of unbearable desire. And yet another. And another. Each one stronger, more urgent than the last.

She wanted this with all her being. Madness though it was. She didn't care—could not care—could only go on yielding endlessly, urgently, to the hunger that was growing in her with every passing moment, every yearning press of her body into his.

And then suddenly, abruptly, his hand was lifted from her—and his mouth. With a muffled cry of loss she tried to reach for him again, her eyes blind to all but the overpowering need for him that had brought her to this point. But he resisted her reach and instead, with a gasp of shock, he flipped her over so her face was pressed into the pillows.

She tried to raise herself.

'Lie still.'

There was a growl in his voice—a growl that melted her bones. For she knew at a level so deep she did not understand it that this was a command that was for her, not him. And a moment later she realised why.

His hands were at the back of her dress and his fingers were working assiduously, steadily, at slipping free the myriad tiny hooks that fastened the exquisite gown. It seemed to take for ever, and she felt herself grow restless, filled with a sense of frustration that it was taking so long for him to ease the delicate fabric from her skin, exposing, hook by hook, the long line of her spine. She felt her fingers clutch at the silk of her pillow, felt a heat building in her—a heat she could not cool, did not want to cool.

She wanted only to feel as she did when finally the fabric fell aside, and then his long velvet fingertips were easing beneath, splaying out with the most leisurely arousing touch, so that her fingers clenched more tightly, the restlessness in her mounting, wanting more of him, more of his feathered touch, more of the way his mouth was now lowering to her spine, grazing each sculpted contour as swirls of pleasure began to ripple through her.

As his lips grazed down her spine, teasing those swirls of exquisite sensation from her, she felt his hands spread out, easing the gown completely from her until it was all but falling off. Gently, but with a strength that made it effortless, he lifted her from the gown so that it lay like a discarded thing beside her. Gently he lowered her back upon the silken divan, turning her towards him.

She was naked—completely naked. For an endless moment he gazed down at her. Incapable of more. Incapable of anything except letting his eyes feast on the incredible beauty of her naked body. She was everything he'd known she would be—everything and more. Oh, *so* much more!

Her slender frame, the narrow waist, the perfect contours, the sweet lushness of her breasts, bared now for him alone. The swell of her hips, the deep vee below, her long legs, her loosening thighs...

Then with a sudden movement he sat up, seizing the priceless gown. She did not even remark when he dropped it to the floor—her eyes were only for him. Urgently he hauled his own clothing from him—so much more swiftly than he'd just freed her from the gown that had done its job so well—had made her aware of her own beauty, of how precious it was to her, to him, and was now no longer necessary.

Nothing was needed now. Now they had everything they wanted. They had the silken couch, the night sky, the warmth of the desert, the silence and the darkness, the stars their only witness.

They had each other.

It was all that he wanted now. All he had wanted from the first moment he had set eyes on her. This exquisitely beautiful woman, so different from any he had known, offering him so much...

Offering him now the greatest gift of all—the gift that he had waited so many months to claim.

Herself.

She was his at last. The ice maiden was gone for ever. His self-control, his self-denial was finally needed no longer and she was melting in his arms.

Melting and then catching fire at his touch, his kiss, his absolute caress.

With a sense of absolute liberty he lowered himself down beside her. Smoothed her golden hair from her forehead. Gazed down at her with a look that told her everything she needed to know, that sent the blood flushing through her, hot and urgent.

'And now,' said Nikos as he started to lower his mouth, his voice rich with anticipation, satisfaction, 'we can begin our wedding night.'

CHAPTER SEVEN

THE SUN WAS RISING, swelling over the rim of the easternmost dune, bleaching the sky, quenching the stars one by one by one. Rose-gold lit up the horizon, a long, rich line of colour as the sky above turned to azure blue.

In Nikos's arms, Diana slept—as he slept in hers. Her head and torso rested on his chest, that strong, muscle-sculpted wall that could take her weight as if she were feathers drifting from a passing eagle. And around her waist his arm was clamped, heavy upon her, but it was a weight she'd gloried in, holding her to him even as sleep had swept over them in the long, late reaches of the night.

A wedding night that had burned hot as the distant stars whose light had illuminated their bodies—bodies moving in passion, in desire, in endless, boundless need and satiation. Her voice had cried out time after time, each note higher with an ecstasy that had ripped her mind from her body then melded them back, fusing them with the same heat that had fused her body to his. Fusing them as if they were one body, one flesh. They had clasped each other, their tangled limbs impossible to separate.

The sun crept higher now, spilling into the day. It shafted the world with brilliant radiance. Washing up over their naked bodies, covered only by the silken cloths with which the divan was strewn.

Diana stirred. There was warmth moving along her legs now, and she wondered why, her eyes flickering feebly open, blinking at the day. The sun had gained its final clearance of the dunes and now blazed out over the rooftop, instantly heating them. She felt Nikos stir too, his limbs tensing as he moved upwards out of deep sleep.

The arm around her tightened automatically. But he did not wake.

Breathless, Diana eased herself from him. Her body was stiff, unyielding, but move she must. Carefully, very carefully, she stood up. Every muscle in her body ached. She cast her gaze about. She could not stand here naked, exposed on the rooftop. She dipped down, seizing up her cashmere shawl and hurriedly swathing it around herself as consciousness increasingly came back to her.

With a smothered cry she pressed the tips of her fingers against her mouth.

What have I done? Oh, what have I done?

But she knew what she had done. The evidence was there, spread out beneath her gaze—a gaze that could not help but instantly go to the powerful male glory of Nikos's naked his body. An amazed delight leapt in her. Flaring through every cell in her body. Firing every synapse in her dazed brain.

I never knew... I just never knew how it could be!

But she knew now. Knew that Nikos had taken her to a place she had never understood, never realised existed. She felt dazed with the knowledge. Stunned by it.

But it was not knowledge that she could possess freely. She felt her stomach plummet. Dear God, what she had done she should never have allowed herself to do. How *could* she?

This was not what she had married Nikos for.

It was not what he'd married *her* for.

That was the blunt truth of it. The truth that crushed her as she hurried barefoot back down to the interior rooms, rushing into the bathroom. Maybe water would sluice away the madness of what she'd done.

But when she finally emerged from her shower, wrapped in a huge towel, it was to find Nikos waiting for her. He didn't speak—not a word. He was wearing a cotton dressing gown now, and he simply strode up to her. Wrapped her to him.

His bear hug was all-enveloping. Impossible to draw back from.

But I don't want to! I don't want to pull away from him.

The cry came from deep within, from a place she had not known existed. Not until last night.

It seemed an age before he let her go, but when he

did he simply said, his eyes alight, his smile wide, 'Breakfast awaits.'

He scooped up a silken robe that was lying draped across the unused bed. It was in sea-green, vivid and vibrant, and he threw it around her and slipped the towel from her.

'You must keep covered,' he growled, and there was an expression in his eyes that she did not need a dictionary to describe. 'Or we'll never get to breakfast.'

His arm around her shoulder, he led her out. She went with him, as meekly as a lamb. For it was the only thing in the world she wanted to do.

Out on the terrace the silent army of servants had set a lavish breakfast table, shaded by an awning, and they took their places. Beyond the terrace and beyond the outdoor pool glittering in the morning sun, the palm trees guarding it, the desert stretched to infinity. All the world was here, in this one place.

In this one man.

Nikos raised his glass of orange juice to her, his smile wide and warm. His eyes warmer still.

'To us, Diana,' he said.

To us? she echoed silently. There was no 'us'— there was only an empty shell of a marriage, designed to make use of each other, with no future in it. None.

But, as she raised her own glass defiance and a reckless daring surged up in her. Beyond this desert hideaway there could be no 'us' for her and Nikos.

But while we are here there can.

And for that... Oh, for that she would seize it all.

* * *

'All strapped in?' Nikos said, checking her seat belt. He nodded at their driver. 'OK, let's go.'

With a roaring gunning of the engine the driver grinned and accelerated the four-by-four almost vertically up the perilous slope of the dune.

Within seconds Diana discovered why it was called 'dune-bashing'. She shrieked and covered her eyes as the skilled driver performed manoeuvres that took them to the top, then slid them down the other side, then careered up again to totter precariously at an impossible angle before plunging down in a huge flurry of sandy and sideways sliding.

Nikos hoped that she was, despite appearances, enjoying herself.

By the time the driver finally screeched to a juddering halt, turning back to Nikos with a triumphant grin on his face, he believed she was.

'Oh, good *grief*!' she cried, half-laughing, half-shaking as she finally let go her death grip on the door strap. 'I was absolutely *terrified*!'

'Me too,' Nikos admitted ruefully.

He turned to the driver, exchanging comments on how he'd performed those almost impossible and certainly potentially lethal manoeuvres on the steep soft sand.

Diana caught at his arm. 'No, Nikos, you are *not* to try doing it yourself!' she exclaimed feelingly.

He turned towards her. 'Worried for me?' he asked, grinning. His eyes glinted. 'How very wifely of you.'

It was lightly said, but it was like a sudden sword

in her side, reminding her of just how little right she had to be 'wifely'. But she could not, *would* not think of that now. Not here in the desert, cocooned in this world so distant from their own.

And then Nikos was announcing his need for lunch—for breakfast had been long ago, before they'd set out to try their hands at the ship of the desert, mounting camels as the patient beasts lay on the sand, clambering up with a serpentine grace and starting to move with their slow, swaying gait.

Diana had found the experience unforgettable as her camel trod silently along the way, feeling only the desert wind playing across her heated cheeks, her head shaded by a wide-brimmed hat, the blown sand off the tops of the dunes catching in the light, the burning azure bowl of the sky arching over them, and the endless ocean of sand stretching boundless and bare all around. She'd felt as if she were in a different world. Ancient and primeval, timeless and eternal.

Far, far away from the real world beyond.

But this world here, now, timeless and primeval, was the world she was giving herself to—and she was giving herself to the man here with her, to this time together. She would not think of the world beyond, would not remember it. Not now.

Elation seared through her—a kind of reckless joy as she seized this moment, this time out of time that had come to her unasked-for, unsought, but which she had taken all the same, bestowed upon her like a gift of all gifts.

The gift of this time with Nikos, the man who, out

of all men that existed, had taken her to a place she had not believed could ever be for her.

But it is—it is! It's real for me—passion and desire. It's real and now I have it—here, with Nikos, in this timeless place.

That was all she cared about, all she would let herself care about, feel and believe. This time *now*, with Nikos, alone in the desert.

She could see the camels again now, lying down in the shade of high rocks, resting, as their four-by-four descended to the level dirt track again, taking her and Nikos to where a canopy had been set up over carpets laid on the sand.

There they were offered moistened, cooling cloths to wipe their dusty hands and hot faces, before tucking into an array of spiced and fragranced dishes whose delicious aroma quickened her appetite.

And not just for food.

Her eyes slid to the man she was with and she felt that rush of amazement and wonder that came every time she looked at him, feasted on him. He caught her open gaze and smiled—a warm, intimate smile that brought colour flushing to her cheeks. He said nothing, though, only let his long lashes sweep down as he urged her to try yet another dish.

Around them servants stood, pouring cool drinks from tall silver jugs, removing empty dishes, replacing them with yet more food that seemed to be arriving in a procession from the open-air cooking station some way down-wind of where they lounged.

Eventually, sated and replete, Diana felt her eyelids start to drift down.

'I'm falling asleep,' she heard herself say as the heat and drowsiness of midday took their soporific toll.

'Then sleep,' said Nikos.

He made a gesture for the servants to clear the last of the bowls and glasses, which they instantly did, then reached across to Diana, drawing her down on the cushions beside him, letting her head loll on his lap. Idly he stroked her hair, plaited into a confining ponytail, but feathering in soft tendrils around her face. Her beautiful, fine-boned face, flushed now with the sun, her hair bleached even paler.

He felt desire stir in him, but held it at bay. It would wait until they were private again.

A slow smile slid across his features and there was reminiscence in his eyes. Their eventual consummation had been everything he'd wanted. Everything he'd intended. Leisurely he replayed in his head that first night—melting her under the stars, seeing the revelation in her starlit eyes as realisation had swept over her, as she'd felt the full intensity of the sensations he'd drawn from her, using all his skills and experience, knowing just what would most sate the desire burning in her like a flame. A desire *he* had kindled, against her own long-held assumption that men were of no sexual interest to her.

His smile deepened, took on a sensual twist. Well, he had made an end of *that*! From now on she would burn for him—burn for however long it took before his desire for her began to wane and the day came when he woke and knew their time together was done with.

Until that time came she was his...

He felt his own lids grow heavy in the somnolent heat. To lie like this, with Diana supine in his lap, her arm across his limbs, warm and close and intimate, was so very good.

Would he *ever* not want her?

The question hung like an eagle over the desert sand, motionless and unanswered, as his eyelids closed and he, too, succumbed to sleep.

'I hate to say this...' Nikos's voice sounded regretful '...but our idyll here is over.'

Diana looked across at him as they sat taking their breakfast in the beautiful inner courtyard, the trickling fountain cooling the air beside them, verdant greenery all around them in the private, enclosed space.

Nikos set down his phone. 'That was the Minister for Development's office. There's another meeting this afternoon with the minister and several other bigwigs. I'll need to be there.'

Diana blinked. The world beyond the desert had seemed so very far away, and yet here it was intruding, downloaded from the ether, summoning them back to reality. She tried to count the days since they'd arrived here from the coast, and failed. One day had segued into the next—indolent, lazy, luxurious, self-absorbed and self-indulgent. A time of passion and desire—a time of bliss.

A fantasy of *Arabian Nights* made real…

And now it was to be ended.

A kind of numb dismay filled her—a sense of dissociation, loss.

Nikos was already getting to his feet. 'I need my laptop,' he said. 'There are some things I must check. Finish your breakfast, though. There is no immediate rush. They're sending a helicopter to take us back to the city.'

The helicopter, when it arrived, was a huge, noisy, angry wasp, churning up the sand, landing just beyond the perimeter fence. It seemed like an invasion to Diana. As Nikos helped her aboard, ducking under the sweeping rotors, it was as if the twenty-first century was crashing back into her.

The machine took off with a deafening roar, wheeling up into the steel-blue sky, casting its wrinkled shadow over the dunes as it headed back to the coast. It took them back to their hotel, but Nikos was not there long—only long enough to shower, change into his business suit, take up his briefcase and depart again, leaving Diana alone and feeling dislocated and bereft in their suite.

Her head was all in pieces. The abrupt change was jarring. From the emptiness of the desert—the absolute privacy of their time there and all that that had brought—back now into the modern world, busy and crowded, demanding and bustling.

Here, time existed. Other people existed. Other priorities. Other realities.

Realities that now forced themselves upon her.

She did not want to face them—but she must.

Restlessly she paced about, netted by tension. There was a deep disquiet within her. A deep, fearful unease.

Danger was lapping at her feet...

CHAPTER EIGHT

NIKOS THREW HIMSELF into the back of his car, his face set. That meeting had *not* gone well. The damned internal politics of the sheikdom were raising their heads again. Sheikh Kamal's cousin, Prince Farouk, who was against *all* development, was leaning on the minister to block him, Nikos, favoured as he was by Sheikh Kamal. So, although the minister had been urbane, he had also been regretful. And adamant.

There would be problems. Difficulties. Delays. It was unfortunate, but there it was.

He gave a frustrated sigh. Sheikh Kamal, shrewd and far-seeing, would, he knew, outmanoeuvre his cousin in the long term, and until then he would have to exercise patience—though it went against the grain to do so. All his life he'd targeted what he wanted, gone after it and achieved it. Wealth, a trophy mistress, and now a trophy wife.

Immediately his mood improved. After all, there was an upside to this delay in his business affairs here. It would give him more time with Diana...

He felt himself start to relax and his body thrummed

with anticipation. She would be waiting for him in their suite, no longer the ice maiden but the warm, ardent, passionate woman of his desires, fully awakened by *him*, as by no other man, to the rich glory of her sensuality.

A sensuality that had swept him away.

Oh, Nadya had been a passionate woman—fiery and tempestuous—and he'd always chosen women for their passion. But with Diana... His expression changed, became wondering. With Diana it had been more than passion, that incandescent union with her beneath the stars.

He tried to understand it, to comprehend it. Was it because he'd had to wait so long to claim her? Was that the reason that those days with her in the desert had been so...so *special*? So different from any other days he'd known? Was it because she'd been that untouchable ice maiden, yielding to him only after so long a wait? An ice maiden only he could thaw, who only melted in *his* arms, no other man's?

A frown drew his brows together as he tried to work it out. Work out why it was that those nights he'd spent with her had been so overwhelming.

Because it wasn't just passion or desire—that was why. There was more than that. Oh, yes, there was a sense of triumph that she'd finally yielded to him and his patience had been so lavishly rewarded. But still there was more than that.

It was the sense of companionship they'd shared. Whether it had been watching the stars, knowing she was as beguiled by their majesty as he was—something that Nadya would have found incomprehensible and irrelevant—or laughing as they'd swayed on those poor camels, bearing the load of riders who were rookies, or leaning back into each other's arms as they lounged on the divans by the poolside, under an awning out in the desert heat.

And talking—always talking. Sometimes about world affairs, sometimes just about anything or nothing. Stimulating and energising, or easy and uncomplicated—they could segue from one to the other effortlessly, seamlessly.

I like her company—I enjoy being with her—whether she is in my arms or just spending time with me.

Was it really that simple? If it was, then there was something else, too. Something basic, fundamental—something he'd never thought about before.

She is happy to be with me. She likes my company...enjoys being with me. As I enjoy being with her—for her company, for just being together...

That seemed an odd thing to think, in many ways, because it wasn't something he'd ever considered before when it came to women. It made him realise that the time he'd spent with Nadya, with all of her predecessors had been entirely superficial. It had been about sex—nothing more than that. Nadya had been specifically chosen to be a trophy mistress—showing the world he could have so lauded and beautiful a woman in his bed, on his arm.

Memory flickered in him. He'd thought of Diana as the next step on from that. Did he still think of her that way? Merely as a trophy wife? Or could the woman he'd made his own beneath the desert stars mean something more to him?

Maybe I'll never get bored with her! Maybe I'll never tire of her?

The thought hovered in his mind. It was something that he'd never felt about any woman before and he did not know the answer—not yet. For now all he wanted was what he had had in the desert—Diana in his arms, clinging to him in ecstasy.

Arriving at the hotel, he strode across the vast atrium, hastening up to the honeymoon suite. To Diana—warm and ardent with all the passion he had awakened in her, all the desire he had released in her.

My bride. My wife!

Emotion washed through him—strange and un-familiar. It was desire for her, yes—strong and powerful—but more than that too. He didn't know what, but it was there, just as strong, just as power-ful. He wondered at it, for he did not recognise it, had no experience of it.

Then the elevator doors were opening, and with eager steps he strode along the plush corridor to reach their suite, swiping the key card and going in.

She was there, by the window of the balcony, a cof-fee tray set out on the dining table in the embrasure where she sat with her tablet, studying the screen. She looked up with a startled expression as he walked in, carelessly tossing aside his briefcase.

'Oh!' she exclaimed.

For a moment there was a panicked look on her

face, but Nikos didn't register it. He walked up to her, loosening his tie as he did so, as if it were constricting him.

'Thank God that's over,' he said feelingly. 'That damned meeting!'

Diana looked at him, alarmed. 'It didn't go well?'

Was there strain in her voice? He hardly knew. Instead he answered directly.

'A set-up by Sheikh Kamal's rival for power,' he expostulated. 'I'm being blocked—and it's because of an internal power struggle in the royal family.'

'Oh, I'm sorry...' Diana's voice was concerned, but distracted.

He shook his head. 'Well, it's not that bad. Things will come about. I put my money on Kamal—he's a smart guy and won't be outmanoeuvred. But I'll have to hold fire for a while.' His expression changed. 'In a way,' he said, and there was a glint in his eye now, 'it has its advantages. Gives me more free time while we're here. We can enjoy ourselves all the more. Starting...' there was a growl in his voice '...right now.'

He drew her upright, made to slide her into his arms, into his waiting embrace. It was good, *so* good to have her here for him. So good to feel her slender body, so pliant, so beautiful, to see her upturned face, her mouth waiting for the kisses which she had come to yearn for in their desert idyll, returning them as ardently as he bestowed them. Diana, his beautiful, exquisite Diana—*his*, all his, completely, all-consumingly.

'I've been aching for you,' he said, his voice a low, husky growl, his eyes alight with sensual desire. 'Aching…'

His mouth lowered to hers, his arms around her tightening. But there was something wrong—something different. She was tensing her body, straining back from him.

'Nikos—'

There was something wrong in her voice, too.

He drew back a moment, loosening his clasp but not relinquishing her. 'What is it?' he said. Concern was in his voice, in the searching frown of his eyes.

She slipped her hands from her sides to rest them against his shoulders—to brace herself against them. Hold herself away.

'Nikos—we…we can't!'

His frown deepened, as did his expression of concern.

'What is it?' he asked again. 'What is wrong?'

She did not answer, then carefully she drew away from him. He let her go and she walked to the far side of the dining table, as if to put it between them.

'We need to talk.'

He stared at her. There was distress in her voice, in her face—her eyes.

His brows drew together in a frown. 'What is it?' he said, and now his voice was different too. Edged.

She took a breath. Cowardice bit within her. And temptation. Sweeping, overpowering temptation! The temptation not to say what she was steeling herself to say. To keep silent. To hold out her arms to Nikos and let him sweep her against him. To carry her through to that preposterous bridal bed smothered in rose petals and take her to the place they had found in each other's arms, each other's ecstasy.

But if she did…

Emotion devoured like the jaws of a wolf. If she succumbed, as she so longed to succumb, then what she had tried to keep at bay out in the desert, what she had denied, refused, would happen.

And I cannot let it happen. I dare not!

All her life she had kept intimacy at bay, kept herself safe from what she had seen destroy her father. The hurt he'd suffered that she dared not risk for herself! So now she must say what she must say. Do what she must do.

Nikos's voice was cutting across her anguished thoughts.

'Diana—speak to me. What is it?'

There was steel in Nikos's voice now. He wanted answers, explanations. Something was going wrong, and he wanted to know what it was. *Why* it was. So that he could fix it. Whatever it was, he could fix it.

Her breath caught—then she forced herself into words. Words she had to say. *Had* to…

'Nikos—what happened in the desert…it shouldn't have happened!'

Disbelief flashed across his face. 'How can you say that?'

His voice was hollow. As if the breath had been punched from his body by a blow that had landed out of nowhere. His mind was reeling, unable to comprehend what she had just thrown at him. It made no sense. *No sense.* How could she possibly be saying what she had just said?

'And how can you *not* see that?' she cried in response. 'It's not what our marriage is about! It never was—it was never anything more than…than convenience! A marriage that would suit us both, provide us both with something that was important to each of us—restoring Greymont for me, an *entrée* into my world for you! And then we'd go our separate ways! You *said* that, Nikos—you said it yourself to me. It was what you proposed!'

She took another ragged breath.

'And that's what I agreed to. *All* I agreed to.'

He was staring at her. Every line in his face frozen. Disbelieving.

'Are you telling me,' he said slowly, 'that you actually believe our marriage should be *celibate*?'

Now it was Diana looking at him as if he were insane. Her eyes flared. 'Of *course*!' she said. 'That's what we signed up to. Right from the start.'

An oath sprang from him. 'I don't believe I'm hearing this!' he said.

His voice was still hollow, but there was an edge to it that made her blench.

He took a heaving breath. Lifted his hands. 'Diana, how can you possibly have thought our marriage should be celibate? When did I *ever* give you cause to think so?'

Consternation filled her features. 'Well, of course I thought you thought that! You gave me every rea-

son to believe so. Nikos, you never laid a finger on
me in all the time of our engagement. Nor when we
first arrived here!'

He ran his hand agitatedly through his hair. He
still could not believe what he was hearing. It was
impossible—just impossible—that she should have
thought what she *said* she'd thought. Impossible!

'I was giving you *time*, Diana. Time to get to know
me, to get used to me. Of *course* I wasn't going to
be crass enough to pounce on you the moment we'd
signed the marriage register. I wanted the time to be
right for us.'

He made no reference to ice maidens—what help
would that have been? She probably hadn't even been
aware that she *was* one—that she'd radiated *Look
but don't touch* as if it had beamed from her in high
frequency.

The very fact that she was talking now, in this insane way, of celibacy—dear God, when they were
married, when they'd just returned from that burning consummation under the desert stars—was proof
of how totally unaware she was of how unaroused,
how frozen she had been. It was a state she'd thought
was normal.

His mind worked rapidly. Was that why she was
being like this now? Was this just panic—a kind of
delayed 'morning after the night before' reaction as
she surfaced back in the real world, away from the
desert idyll that had so beguiled her—beguiled them
both? That must be it—it was the only explanation.

His mood steadied and he forced himself to stay

calm. Reasonable. He took a breath, lowering his voice, making it sound as it needed to now. Reassuring.

'And we *have* come to know each other, haven't we, Diana?' he went on now, in that reassuring tone. 'We've got used to one another now that we've finally had time to be with each other, now we're married—and we've found each other agreeable, haven't we? We get on well.'

His expression changed without him being aware of it. It was vital that she understood what he was saying now.

'Maybe if we hadn't had that invitation from the Sheikh to stay at his desert palace it might have taken longer for our relationship to deepen. To reach the conclusion that it has. A conclusion, Diana, that has *always* been inevitable.'

He took a step towards her, unconscious of his action, only of his need to close the distance between them. To make everything all right between them again. The way it had been in the desert.

His voice was husky. He had to tell her. He had to make things clear to her, cut through the confusion that must be in her, the panic, even, which was the only way he could account for what she was saying.

'It's always been there, Diana, right from the start. That flame between us. Oh, it was hardly visible at first—I know that—but I know, too, that you were not indifferent to me, however much you might have been unaware of it at a conscious level. And, Diana…' his voice dropped '…believe me, I was the very opposite of indifferent to you from the very moment I first saw you. But it took the desert, Diana, to let that invisible flame that has always run between us flare into the incandescent fire that took us both.'

He strode around the table. Clasped his hands around her shoulders. Gazed down into her face. Her taut and stricken face. He ached to kiss her, to sweep her up into his arms and soothe the panic from her, to melt it away in the fire of his desire—of *her* desire.

'We can't deny what's happened, and nor should we. *Why* should we? We're man and wife—what better way to seal that than by yielding to our passion for each other? The passion you feel as strongly as I do. As powerfully. As irresistibly.'

His voice was low, his mouth descending to hers. He saw her eyelids flutter, saw a look almost of despair in them, but he made himself oblivious to it. Oblivious to everything except the soft exquisite velvet of her lips.

He drew her to him, sliding his hand around her nape, cradling the shape of her head, holding her for his kiss—a kiss that was long and languorous, sensual and seductive. He felt the relief of having her in his arms again, of making everything all right. It was a kiss to melt away her panic, her fears. To soothe her back into his embrace.

He heard the low moan in her throat that betokened, as he now knew, the onset of her own arousal—an arousal he knew well how to draw from her, to enhance with every skilled and silken touch. His hand slid from her shoulder to close his over her breast, which ripened at his touch, the coral peak straining beneath his gentle, sensuous kneading. He groaned low in his chest, feeling his own arousal surge. Desire soared in him—and victory. Victory over her fears, her anxieties. He was melting the ice that was seeking to freeze her again, to take her from him. To lock her back into a snow-cold body, unfeeling, insensate.

He would never let her be imprisoned in that icy fastness again! In his arms he would melt away the last of her fears. The ice maiden was never to return.

He heard again that low moan in her throat and he deepened his kiss, drawing her hips against him, letting her know how much he desired her and how much *she* desired him.

The low moan came again—and then, as her head suddenly rolled back, it became a cry. Her face was convulsing.

'Nikos! *No!*'

He let her go instantly. How could he hold her when she had denied him?

She was backing away, stumbling against the edge of the mahogany table, warding him off with her hand. Her face was working…she was trying to get control of her emotions. Emotions that were searing through her like sheet metal, glowing white-hot. Emotions she had to quench now—right now.

He talks of a flame between us as if that makes it better—it doesn't! It makes it worse—much, much worse! It makes it terrifyingly dangerous! Just as I've feared all my life!

So whatever it took, however much strength she

had to find—desperately, urgently—she had to keep him at bay. *Had* to!

'I don't want this,' she said. Her voice was thin, almost breaking, but she must not let it break. 'I don't want this,' she said again. 'What happened in the desert was a…a mistake. A *mistake*,' she said bleakly.

There was silence—complete silence. She took another razoring breath, then spoke again, her voice hollow. Forcing herself to say what she *had* to say.

'Nikos, if I had thought…realised for one moment that you intended our marriage to be anything but a marriage in name only, that you intended it to be consummated, I would never have agreed to marry you.'

Her jaw was aching, the tension in her body unbearable, but speak she must. She had to make it crystal-clear to him.

'It wasn't why I married you.'

She forced herself to hold his gaze. There was something wrong with his face, but she could not say what. Could do nothing but feel the emotions within her twisting and tightening into vicious coils, crushing the breath from her.

The silence stretched, pushing them apart, repelling them from each other.

As they must be.

There was incomprehension in his eyes. More than that. Something dark she did not want to see there that chilled her to the bone.

Then he was speaking. The thing that was wrong in his face, in his eyes, was wrong in his voice, too. It had taken on a vicious edge of sarcasm that cut into her with a whip-like lash.

'I thank you for your enlightening clarification about our marriage,' he said, and coldness iced inside him. 'In light of which it would therefore be best if you returned to the UK immediately. Tonight. I will make the arrangements straight away.'

He turned, and with a smothered cry she made to step after him.

'Nikos! Please—don't be like that. There's no need for me to leave. We can just be as we were before…'

Her voice trailed off. The words mocked her with the impossibility of what she was saying.

We can never be as we were before.

His face had closed. Shutting her out as if an iron gate had slammed down across it.

'There is no purpose in further exchange. Go and pack.'

He was walking away, picking up the house phone on the sideboard, uttering the brief words necessary to set in motion her departure.

'I have work to do,' he said.

His voice was as curt as it had been to the person at the front desk. He walked over to where he'd tossed his briefcase, picked it up. Walked into the spare bedroom.

She heard the door snap shut.

Then there was silence.

Silence all around her.

CHAPTER NINE

BLACK, COLD ANGER filled Nikos. Like dark ink, it filled his veins, his vision. His gaze, just as dark, was fixed on the blackening cloudscape beyond the unscreened porthole of the first-class cabin of the jet, speeding into the night as far and as fast as it could take him.

Australia would do—the other side of the world from Diana.

Diana whom he had made his wife in good faith. Concealing nothing from her, having no hidden agenda.

Unlike his bride. His oh-so-beautiful ice maiden, his look-but-don't-touch bride, who'd never intended, even from the start, to make their marriage work.

Over and over in his head, like a rat in a trap, he heard that last exchange with her. Telling him what she thought of him. What she wanted of him.

What she did not want.

Not him—no, never that.

'It wasn't why I married you.'

Her words—so stark, so brutally revealing—had told him all. All that she wanted.

Only my money, in order to give her what she wants most in all the world.

His eyes hardened like steel, like obsidian—black and merciless. Merciless against him. Against her.

And what she wants most in all the world is not me.

It was her house—her grand, ancestral home—and the lifestyle that went with it. That was all that was important to her. Not him. *Never* him.

Memory, bitter and acid, washed in his veins, burning and searing his flesh. A memory he could not exorcise from his mind. Driving up to that gracious Normandy chateau bathed in sunlight, so full of hope! Hope that now he was no longer a child, and now he had been told who his parents were by the lawyer who had summoned him to his offices on his eighteenth birthday, he had found the mother who had given him away at birth.

He had been hoping he would discover that there was some explanation for why she had disowned him—something that would unite them, finally, that would see her opening her arms to him in joy and welcome.

His mouth twisted, his face contorting. There had been no joy, no welcome. Only cold refusal, cold rejection. He'd been sent packing.

All I was to her was a threat—a threat to her aristocratic lifestyle. To the lifestyle that came with her title, her grand ancestral home. That was all she wanted. All that was important to her.

The revelation had been brutal.

As brutal as the revelation his wife, his bride, had just inflicted upon him.

He tore his mind away as anger bit again, and beneath the anger he felt another emotion. One he would not name. Would not acknowledge. For to acknowledge it would infect his blood with a poison he would never be able to cleanse it from. Never be free of again.

The jet flew on into the night sky.

Out of the brightness of the day into the dark.

The taxi from the train station made its slow way along the rutted drive that led up to Greymont. The state of the drive was still on her 'to-do' list like a great deal else—including all the interior décor and furnishing work, conserving curtains and restoring ceilings. But the majority of the essential structural work was nearing completion, and work on the electrics and the plumbing were well underway.

Yet the very thought of them burned like fire on Diana's skin.

How could I have got it so wrong? So disastrously, catastrophically wrong!

The question went round and round in her tired, aching head as she walked into her bedroom, collapsed down upon her bed. It had been going round and round ever since she'd walked out of the hotel and into waiting car waiting to take her to the airport, her suitcase having been packed by the maids, her ticket all arranged.

Nikos had stayed immured in his room, the door

locked against her. Refusing to have anything more to do with her. Sending her away.

She'd walked out of the hotel like a zombie, feeling nothing. Nothing until she'd taken her seat on the plane and faced up to what the reality of her marriage was.

Completely and utterly different from what Nikos had thought it would be.

That was what she could not bear. That all along Nikos had assumed their oh-so-mutually convenient marriage was going to include oh-so-mutually convenient sex...

He'd assumed that from the start! Intended it from the start!

And she'd blinded herself to it. Wilfully, deliberately, not wanting to admit that right from that very first moment she'd seen him looking at her it had been with desire.

I told myself he was just assessing me, deciding whether I would fit the bill for his trophy wife, if had the right connections, the right background— the right ancestral home.

Bitter anger at herself writhed within her. How could she have been such a fool not to have realised what Nikos had assumed would be included in their marriage deal? What he'd taken for granted would be included right from the start.

But it was easy to see why. Because she'd wanted to believe that her only role in his life would be to give him an entrée into her upper-class world. Because that had meant she would be able to yield to the desperate temptation that he'd offered her—the means of saving Greymont.

It meant I could take his money and get what I wanted. Easily and painlessly. Safely.

Without any danger to herself.

A smothered cry came from her and she forced her fist into her mouth to keep it from happening again.

Danger? She had wanted to avoid danger—the danger she'd felt from that very first moment of realising that of all the men she had ever encountered it was Nikos Tramontes who possessed the power she had feared all her life.

I walked right into the lion's den. Blindly and wilfully.

And now she was being eaten alive.

The smothered cry came again.

What have I done? Oh, what have I done?

But she knew—had known it the moment she'd surfaced on that rooftop, in the arms of the man she should never have yielded to. She had committed the greatest and most dangerous folly of her life.

Into her head that old saying came: *Take what you want, says God. Take it and pay for it.*

Her eyes stared out bleakly across her familiar childhood room, where she had learned to fear what she must always fear... Well, now she was starting to pay.

Tears welled in her eyes. Anguish rose in her heart.

Nikos was back in London. He'd spent three weeks in Australia, returning to Europe via Shanghai, and then spent another week in Zurich. He had, he thought grimly, been putting off going to London. But he could not put it off for ever.

When he arrived at his house in Knightsbridge his expression darkened. He'd imagined bringing Diana here after their honeymoon, carrying her over the threshold, taking her to bed...

Well, that would not happen now. Would never happen. The black, dark anger that he was now so familiar with, that seemed always to be there now when he thought of her—which was all the time—swilled in his veins. His mouth set in a hard line.

He reached for his phone. Dialled her number. It went to voicemail, and he was glad of it. He did not want to hear her voice.

His message was brief. 'I'm in London. I require you. Be here tomorrow. We have an evening party to go to.'

He disconnected, his expression masked. Diana—his wife, his bride—might have made clear what she thought of him, what she thought of their marriage, but that was of no concern to him right now. She had duties to perform. Duties he was paying her to perform.

However reluctant she might be to do so.

Diana arrived, as summoned, at the end of the following afternoon. The housekeeper admitted her. Nikos was still at his London offices, but he arrived shortly afterwards. She had installed herself in a bedroom that was very obviously *not* the master bedroom. She'd brought a suitcase with her and was hanging up her clothes—including several evening dresses.

As he walked in she started, and paled.

'Nikos—'

There was constraint in her voice, in her face—in her very stance. Yet the moment her eyes had lit upon him she had felt the disastrous, betraying leap of her blood.

He ignored her, walked up to the wardrobe she was filling with her gowns and leafed through them, extracting one and tossing it on the bed.

'Wear this,' he instructed. 'Be ready to leave in an hour.'

He walked out again.

Behind him, Diana quailed. She had dreaded coming up to town, dreaded seeing him again, but knew she had to. Could not evade it. Could not hide at Greymont any longer.

I have to talk to him—stop him being like this. Try to make it like it was originally between us—civil, friendly...

The words mocked her. Agitation and worse, much worse, churned inside her.

Joining him in the drawing room, changed into the gown he wanted her to wear, steeling herself, she felt them mock her again. He was wearing evening dress, tall and dark and devastating, and as her eyes lit on him a ravening hunger went through her, blood leaping in her veins. She almost ran towards him, to throw herself into his arms, to hold him tight.

Memories exploded in her head of herself in his arms, he in hers…

She thrust them from her.

I cannot let myself desire him.

Desperately she schooled herself to quench that perilous leaping of her blood, the flood of memories in her head. Too dangerous.

He turned his head at her entry, and for just a second she thought she saw the briefest flaring of his eyes as they alighted on her. Then the light was extinguished. He let his gaze rest on her.

'Very suitable,' he said.

His voice was flat, his face closed. She made herself walk towards him, his chill gaze still upon her, feeling the swish of her silken gown around her legs, the low coil of the chignon at her nape, the cool of her pearl necklace around her throat. On the little finger of her left hand her signet ring glinted in the lamp light—the St Clair family crest outlined. A perpetual reminder of why she had become his wife—to keep the house that went with this armorial crest.

She fancied she saw Nikos's shuttered gaze flicker to it, then away.

'Nikos…' She made herself speak, lifting her chin to give her courage—courage she did not feel, feeling only a hollow space inside her. 'Nikos, we have to talk.'

He cast her a crushing look. 'Do we? Have you yet more to tell me, Diana?'

There was a harshness in his voice she had never

heard before. An indifference. Absently he busied himself adjusting his cufflinks, not looking at her.

She swallowed again, her throat tight. 'Look, Nikos, our marriage was a mistake. A misunderstanding. I'm sorry—so very sorry—that I got it so wrong in understanding what you…' She swallowed again. 'What you expected of it.'

She couldn't look him in the eyes. It was impossible. He wasn't saying anything, so she went on. Making herself continue. Say the next thing she had to say.

'I've stopped the work on Greymont.'

She said it in a rush, her eyes flying to him, but he gave no indication that he had heard, only went on inspecting his cuff. If she'd thought she saw a nerve work in his taut cheek she must have been mistaken.

She took another breath.

'I've made a tally of all that has been done so far, and anything I'm contracted for. But everything else has been halted. As for what has already been done—the total sum it amounts to…' She faltered, then made herself go on. 'I will do my best to repay you. It will take time—a lot of time, because if I had been able to raise the capital myself I would have done so. And if I realise all my capital, sell my stocks and shares, I'll lose the income from them that I need for maintenance. That's always been the problem—trying to find money both for the restoration and simply keeping Greymont going. The maintenance costs are high—from local taxes to utilities, to just keeping everything ticking over. The place has to be heated in winter or damp gets in, and rot. And I can't throw the Hudsons out on to the street…'

She was rambling, trying to make him understand. He simply went on not looking at her.

'But I will repay you, Nikos. However long it takes me.'

He looked at her then. Finally spoke. 'Yes, you *will* repay me, Diana, of that I am certain.'

She paled. There was something in his voice that felt like a blow. Her lips were dry, but she made herself speak. Tried to reach him.

'Nikos, I'm sorry! I'm sorry this has gone so wrong. I blame myself—I was naïve, stupid. I really thought you wanted a marriage in name only—'

'What I *want*, Diana—' his voice cut across hers like a guillotine '—is for you to honour your agreement with me. To make your repayment in the only way you can. The only way I want you to.'

The blood drained from her face and she seemed to sway. He saw it and wanted to laugh. A savage, baiting laugh. Emotions were scything through him, slicing and slicing. She was standing so close. A single step would take him to her. Crush her to him.

But she was beyond him now. Beyond him for ever.

His expression changed. Became mocking. Savagely mocking. Mocking himself.

'It's what you signed up for, Diana. To be—what did you call yourself? Ah, yes. My "society wife". At my side, graceful and poised, beautiful and elegant—the envy of other men, a trophy on my arm, with your impeccable background, your absolute self-assurance in how to conduct yourself, whether in palaces or in stately homes, or anywhere else I take you. Opening a door for me into your upper-class world. And that's what you will do, Diana, my chaste and beautiful bride.'

His face was set, grim now.

'It will be your full-time job. If you've halted restoration work on Greymont, so much the better. It will give you all the time you require to do your work here, at my side. Starting…' he glanced at his watch '…right now.'

He crossed to the door and opened it, pointedly waiting for her to walk through. As she did so she strained away from him, and he saw that she did. Saw that she was as tense as a board, her features taut. He didn't care. Would not care. Would do nothing at all but steer her to the front door.

As he opened it he turned to her. 'I'll brief you in the car about where we are going, who our hosts are and why they are important to me.'

His tone was businesslike, crisp. And as remote as a frozen planet.

She could not look at him. Could only feel a stone forming in her throat, like a canker growing inside her. Melding to her flesh. Choking her.

The house in Regent's Park was lit up like a Christmas tree, but for Diana it was dark and cheerless. She stood, wine glass in hand, her drink untouched and a stiff smile on her face, and forced herself through the ritual of polite chit-chat that the occasion required.

Nikos was standing beside her. Occasionally his arm would brush against hers, and she had to try not to flinch visibly.

He was no longer the person she'd thought she had come to know. He'd become a stranger—a stranger who spoke to her with chilly impersonality, looking at her but not meeting her eyes, withdrawing behind an expressionless mask. She'd had no option but to do likewise and play the part he wanted her to play—Mrs Nikos Tramontes, the oh-so-elegant, oh-so-well-bred, oh-so-well-connected society wife, with her impeccable background and her magnificent stately home—the home her husband's vast wealth had saved for her.

Exactly the marriage she had wanted.

Take what you want...take it and pay for it.

The words mocked her with a cruelty that she had never thought they could possess.

I brought this on myself! I did it to myself! Fool that I am!

A memory as blazing as the desert stars sought entry, but she held it at bay with all her remaining strength. To remember... No, no, she could not bear it! Could not bear to think of what she should never have permitted herself to have.

It had left her here, now, in this hollow shell of a marriage she should never have made, mocking her with bitter gall. Demanding a price from her that was anguish in every way. And she must go on paying, go on enduring...

* * *

Over the weeks that followed—weeks that were spent at Nikos's side, at his direction, on his requirement, she played her part. Performing her social role as Mrs Nikos Tramontes, immaculately dressed whatever the occasion, behaving just as the situation demanded, whether it was luncheon parties at Thames-side mansions, cocktail parties in Mayfair, dinners in top restaurants in London or attending the theatre or opera at Nikos's side. Always she was there, always perfect, always smiling. The perfect wife.

Trapped in a marriage that had become a torment and an agony.

Nikos was angry. He was angry all the time now. With the same dark, cold anger that had possessed him when he'd sent Diana—his beautiful, enticing wife, his beautiful, *untouchable* wife—back to what she loved most of all in her privileged world. Her grand house and the gracious lifestyle that went with it, all that was important to her.

As the weeks passed a kind of pall settled over him. Outwardly he went through the motions of life, but it was only for show. Deadness was filling him. Numbing him. With part of his mind he knew he should let Diana go, that it was achieving nothing but torment keeping her in their impossible marriage, and yet letting her go seemed even worse.

He could not face it.

It wasn't supposed to be like this!

His marriage should have given him everything that he wanted! *Everything.* Diana, his trophy wife, would grant him the place in the world his mother's rejection of him had denied him. Diana, so elegantly beautiful, so perfect a wife, would show him off to the world.

And Diana, his ice maiden, would melt for him and him alone...

And now she had brutally, callously rejected him—refused him.

He felt that perpetual anger bite again. Oh, he had his trophy wife, all right, chained to his side, but it was like dust and ashes in his mouth.

She melted in my arms, burned in my embrace under the desert stars! I thought that it was me that she wanted! How could I not have thought that after what we were to each other those precious days? Those days that seemed to bring us so close together—in body and in even more than that.

Into his head came the memory of what he'd felt that day he'd rushed back to her from that disastrous meeting with the Minister for Development, and the question that had formed in his head of what Diana might be to him...more than he had ever envisaged. What she might yet be to him...

He had not answered the question. But now he knew the answer for the savage mockery that it was.

A silent snarl convulsed in his throat. Fool— arrant fool that he'd been! Fool to think he'd melted her. There was nothing in her to melt—not at the core of her. Nothing at all. At the core of her being was only one thing, the only thing she wanted and the only thing she valued.

And it was not him.

All she wanted was to preserve her precious life-style, her grand ancestral home—that was all that was important to her!

It's all she values.

Just as it was all his mother had valued.

Not me.

And his wife—his glitteringly beautiful, icily cold, frozen-to-the-core trophy wife Diana—was the same. The same as the woman who had thrust him from her chateau, ordering him away. Rejecting him.

Just as Diana had.

That was the truth slamming into him day after punishing day. It burned in him like acid in his throat, in his guts. Eating him alive.

He could feel it now, biting invisibly as it always did, by day and by night, as he stood, an untouched glass of champagne in his hand, at this reception at the headquarters of a French investment bank in Paris by whom he was being wooed as a prospective client.

The valuable business he might potentially bring guaranteed that he had the full attention of one of the top directors, but as they talked about business opportunities his mind had scarcely been on the conversation.

He tore his thoughts away. Forced himself to focus on what the director was saying to him.

With a flicker in his eyeline he became aware of someone else coming up to them. A man older than himself by a few years, obviously French, and... Nikos felt his eyes narrow suddenly. He looked vaguely familiar. Did he know him?

The man came up to him, politely but pointedly waiting while the bank's director finished speaking. Then he interjected.

'Monsieur Tramontes, I wonder if I might have a word with you?'

He must be someone notable, for immediately the bank director made a murmuring conclusion and took his leave.

Nikos turned his attention to the man who had addressed him, trying to place him. 'Have we met?' he asked, with an enquiring look and a slight civil smile.

The man did not smile in return. 'No,' he said with a shake of his head.

Nikos frowned. 'Forgive me, you seem familiar…'

The man nodded, acknowledging the comment. He reached inside his jacket pocket, took out a silver card case and extracted a card. He proffered it to Nikos.

'This may account for it,' he said.

Nikos took the card, glanced down at it.

And froze.

All thoughts of Diana, his cold, frozen trophy wife, vanished.

CHAPTER TEN

DIANA WAS IN the rose garden, cutting blooms. Summer sun slanted through the trees that sheltered Greymont from the world beyond, birdsong twittered overhead, and a woodpigeon pecked hopefully nearby. Warmth enveloped her—and peace.

But not in her heart. Not in her soul. Only torment filled her.

How long can I bear this?

Two years, Nikos had told her, holding her to the damning contract she had made—made when she had not known the price she would have to pay, when she had not realised the danger in which she stood, deluding herself, never dreaming she would not be able to bear to pay, but must. Two endless years to endure this hideous, bitter existence. Chained to a husband she had once thought a gift from heaven, who was now keeping her in this hell.

Her only respite was the time she could spend here, at Greymont, when Nikos went abroad and did not want her at his side. Then and only then was she allowed to flee back here, take consolation in the refuge it offered her.

The irony was biting—it was *because* of Greymont that she was trapped in her tormented mockery of a marriage to Nikos. A marriage she could not escape for it was the price she was paying to keep Greymont, to keep it safe.

And safe it was. That was her only comfort. Yes, she had halted all the repairs, but the most critical work had already been completed. The structure of the house was secure, and that was her greatest relief. As for the rest of it—well, she could not even think that far…not yet, not now. Perhaps in the distant future, when she had finally freed herself from Nikos, she would be free…

Free?

The word mocked her, sliding a knife into her flesh.

She could never be free of him.

It was too late.

With a smothered cry she went on cutting, placing the scented blooms—their petals so perfect, so fragrant, so beautiful—into the willow basket at her feet, then, sufficient gathered, she headed indoors. She would arrange them for the drawing room, a task she always found solace in.

But as she left the rose garden and glanced down the long driveway curving far away along the rising ground towards the distant lodge gates she paused, frowning. Two cars were heading along the drive. She could just make them out through the lime trees bordering the avenue. Both cars were long and black, with tinted windows.

Who on earth…? She wasn't expecting anyone.

She made her way indoors, through the garden

room door, hastily depositing the blooms in water but not pausing to arrange them. Then she washed her hands and went out into the hallway to open the front door, not troubling to call for Hudson to do so.

She stepped out on to the wide porch. As she did so the two cars drew up in front of the house and immediately the one behind disgorged a handful of dark-suited men, looking extremely businesslike. A moment of fear struck Diana, then astonishment. One of them came up to her, and as he spoke she realised they were all of Middle Eastern appearance.

'Mrs Tramontes?'

She nodded, and then, with another ripple of astonishment, saw that one of the men was opening the passenger door of the first car, and someone was emerging. A woman who was sailing up to her, imperiously dismissing the dark-suited men who backed away dutifully, still scanning the environment as if sharpshooters might be lurking on her roof.

A gasp escaped Diana—she could not help it. 'Your Highness!' she heard herself exclaim, with open astonishment and incredulity in her voice.

'My dear Mrs Tramontes!'

Princess Fatima greeted Diana warmly. Then she turned to another woman, who had now emerged from the huge dark-windowed car, saying something to her in rapid Arabic. The other woman—chaperon, maid, lady-in-waiting? Diana wondered wildly—glided up to the front door, pressed it open, and then stood aside to admit the Princess.

Helplessly Diana followed suit, wondering what

the bodyguards—as she now realised these men must be—would do. Her attention was all on the Princess, who was now addressing her again.

'I hope you will not mind my unexpected arrival, my dear Mrs Tramontes,' Princess Fatima was saying, 'but I could not resist paying you an afternoon call!'

Diana gathered her manners. Seeing the Princess again was overwhelming—releasing a storm of memories and emotions. With an effort she made herself say what had to be said, while inside her head everything seemed to be falling into a million pieces.

'I'm honoured and delighted, Your Highness,' she said mechanically, forcing a welcoming smile to her lips. Then she shook her head. 'But, alas, I am quite unprepared—you will find my hospitality very poor.'

The Princess waved an airy hand, dismissing her apology. 'The fault is mine for not giving you notice,' she said.

She was looking around, gazing up at the marble staircase, the walls lined with paintings, the cavernous hall fireplace.

'Your house is as beautiful as you told me it was,' she said, her voice warm. 'I am eager to see it all.'

'Of course, Your Highness,' Diana assented faintly.

'But first, would it be too much to hope that I might partake of afternoon tea with you?'

Immediately calling on all her training to behave impeccably, whatever tumult was inside her, Diana assured her it would not be too much to hope at all, and ushered the Princess into the drawing room. Hudson was hovering in the doorway and Diana instructed that tea must to be served by Mrs Hudson, and, please, she was to bake fresh scones.

Back in the drawing room, Princess Fatima was settling down on a sofa. The other woman was standing by the windows looking out, almost as if on guard.

The Princess turned to Diana. 'How very good it is to be here,' she said warmly. 'Please do be seated,' she invited.

Diana sat down on the sofa opposite, her limbs nerveless, and Princess Fatima launched into an enthusiastic panegyric of the charms of Greymont, then graciously accepted the arrival of Mrs Hudson with the tea tray.

'Ah, scones. Delicious!' she exclaimed enthusiastically, and Diana murmured her thanks to the housekeeper for having baked them in record time.

The Princess ate as enthusiastically as she praised, chattering all the while—to Diana's abject relief, for she felt utterly unequal to conversing. She told Diana about the progress being made on the English country house that her brother the Sheikh had bought for her, and expressed absolute delight in the gift Diana had made to her of a historic costume—a mid-eighteenth-century heavily embroidered silk gown with wide panniers—that she planned to display in her private sitting room.

As she expressed her delight shadows fleeted across the polite expression on Diana's face. Memory as vivid as poison stung through her, of she and

Nikos discussing what gift she should make the Princess as they returned from the royal palace.

Pain twisted inside her. It was hard, brutally hard to see the Princess again, to be reminded with bitter acid in her veins of the wedding gift she and Nikos had been given. The gift of the Sheikh's desert love-nest.

More memory seared inside her—unbearable yet indelible.

Had the Princess caught that fleeting shadow? All Diana knew was that as they finished their repast the Princess gave a brief instruction to the veiled woman—servant, lady-in-waiting, chaperone, female bodyguard?—and the woman bowed and left the room.

Only then did the Princess turn to Diana and, in a voice quite different from her gay chatter, asked, 'My dear, what is wrong?'

Diana tensed. 'Wrong, Your Highness?' She tried to make her voice equable, as it had been during their social chit-chat just now.

But Princess Fatima held up an imperious hand, her rings and bracelets flashing in the afternoon sunlight. 'There is a sadness in your face that should not be there. It was not there when we first met. What has put it there?'

Her dark eyes held Diana's grey ones, would not let them go.

'Tell me,' she said. It was half an invitation—half a command. 'I insist.'

And Diana, to her horror and mortification, burst into tears.

* * *

Nikos's expression closed like a stone as he stared down at the gilt-edged card in his hand, read the name on it.

'We have nothing to say to each other,' he bit out.

He made to walk away, but his arm was caught.

'But *I* have much to say to *you*!' the other man said.

There was hauteur in his voice, but there was something else as well. Something that made Nikos stop.

The man's eyes—almost as dark as Nikos's, and as long-lashed—bored into his. Refusing to let Nikos go. The next words the man spoke turned him to stone.

'Our mother wishes to see you—'

Instantly Nikos's face contorted. 'I have no mother.' The savagery in his voice was bitter.

Emotion flashed in the other man's eyes. This man who was his half-brother—son of the woman who had given birth to Nikos, a bastard child, unwanted and unacknowledged, thrust away from her unloving arms, given away to foster parents, spurned and discarded.

The other man was implacable. 'That may soon be truer than you know,' he said, his voice grim. He took a breath, addressed Nikos squarely. 'She is about to have an operation that is extremely risky. She may well not survive. For that reason...' Something changed in his voice—something that Nikos recognised but would not acknowledge. 'For that reason I have agreed to seek you out. Bring you to her.'

Nikos's expression twisted. 'Are you *insane*?' he

said, his voice low, enraged. 'She threw me out when I tried to see her. Refused to accept me. Refused even to admit that she *was* my mother!'

Pain flashed across the other man's face. His own half-brother. A stranger. Nothing more than that.

'There are things I must tell you,' he said to Nikos. 'Must make clear to you. Mostly they concern my father.' He paused. 'My *late* father.'

Dimly Nikos's mind clicked into action. The card that this man—this unknown half-brother—had given him.

He lifted it to glance at it again. Read what it said in silvered sloping engraved script.

Le Comte du Plassis

He frowned. But if this man was the Count—?

'My father is dead,' his half-brother told him. 'He died three months ago. And that is why…' He paused, looked at Nikos. 'That is why everything has changed. Why there are things I need to tell you. Explain.' He took a breath. 'Where can we talk in private?'

He took another breath—a difficult one, Nikos could tell.

'It is essential that we do so.'

For a long, timeless moment Nikos looked at him. Met the dark eyes that were so familiar in the face that was as familiar as his own. Slowly, grimly, he gave his assent.

Inside his chest his lungs were tight, as if bound in iron bars.

* * *

Diana was still sobbing. She was appalled at herself, but could not stop. The Princess had crossed from her sofa to plump herself down beside her, pick up her hands and press them.

'Oh, my dear friend—what is wrong?' She patted Diana's hands, her dark eyes huge with sympathy and concern.

Helpless to stop herself, Diana let all her anguish pour out in a storm of weeping. Gradually it abated, leaving her drained, and she reached for a box of tissues from a magazine holder by the fireplace, mopped at her face mumbling apologies.

'I'm sorry. *So* sorry!' Dear God, how could she have burst into tears like that in front of the Princess? Was she insane to have done such a thing?

But Princess Fatima did not seem either offended or bemused. Only intensely sympathetic. She leant back, indicating that Diana must do the same. Then poured her a new cup of tea with her own royal hands and offered it to Diana, who took it shakily.

'You must tell me everything,' the Princess instructed. 'What has gone wrong between you and your handsome husband? No, don't tell me it hasn't. For I will not believe you. No new wife weeps for any other reason.'

Yet still Diana could not speak. Could only gulp at her tea, then set it down again with still shaky hands. She stared at her royal guest with a blank, exhausted stare.

The Princess took a delicate sip of her own tea and

replaced the cup with graceful ease on the table. Then she spoke, slowly and carefully, looking directly at Diana, holding her smeared gaze.

'Here in the west,' she began, her tone measured, but meaningful, 'I am well aware that it is the custom for marriages to be based on emotion. Love, as you would call it. It is the fashion, and it is the expectation. But for all that it is not always the case, is it?'

Her eyes were holding Diana's fixedly.

'You will forgive me for speaking in a way that you Europeans with your propensity for democracy might find old-fashioned, but for those who are born into responsibilities greater than the acquisition of their own happiness such a custom may not always be appropriate.'

She smiled, exchanging another speaking glance with her hostess.

'Perhaps we are not so unalike, you and I? At some point I must make a marriage for reasons greater than my own personal concerns—and perhaps that is something that you yourself can understand? Something you have also done?'

She patted Diana's hand again, holding her gaze questioningly as she did so.

'I teased you when you visited me,' she reminded Diana, 'about having so handsome a husband that surely he must be the most important aspect of your life— more important than anything else. But perhaps...' She paused, then went on, glancing around her. 'Perhaps that is not so? You gave me reason to suppose that when you answered me...'

Diana's eyes dropped and she stared into her lap. Spoke dully as she replied. With heaviness in her voice.

'I thought I was saving my house…my home. It is dearer to me than anything in the world. I thought—' she gave a little choke '—I thought I would do anything to save it.'

She lifted her eyes, met those of the Princess who, perhaps alone of anyone she knew, would understand.

'Even marry for it.' She took a breath, felt it as tight as wire around her throat. 'So that's what I did. I married to save my house, my home, my inheritance. To honour what my father had done for me.'

She gave the Princess a sad, painful smile.

'My mother left my father when I was a child, but he chose never to remarry. It was for *my* sake. You will not need me to tell you that in England it is the tradition for sons to inherit family estates, not daughters— unless there is no son. My father knew how much I loved Greymont, how important it had become to me. It gave me the sense of security, of continuity, I so desperately needed after my mother abandoned and rejected me. So he gave up his chance of happiness to ensure mine.'

She sighed.

'When he died, and I found I needed so much money to honour his sacrifice for me, I made the decision to marry money. Forgive me,' she said tightly, 'for such vulgar talk—but without money Greymont would eventually decay into a ruin. You know that,

Your Highness, from your own house that you are saving.'

The Princess nodded. 'So you married the handsome man who just happened to have the wealth that you required for this?' She gestured all around her. She paused, then, 'It does not sound so absurd a decision. It was a marriage that made sense, no? Your husband ensured the future of your home and you, my dear Mrs Tramontes, provided the beauty that any husband must treasure!' She paused again, her eyes enquiring. 'So, what is it that has gone so very wrong?'

She searched Diana's face.

Diana, filled with misery, crumpled the sodden tissue in her hands, meshing her fingers restlessly.

'I thought… I thought he married me out of self-interest. Just as I had married him! Because we were *useful* to each other. I—I thought,' she said, her voice faltering, 'that was the only reason and that it would be enough. But then—' She broke off, gave a cry. 'Oh, Your Highness,' she said in anguish, 'your kindness, your brother's generosity, worked magic that was disastrous for me! Disastrous because—'

She felt silent. Incapable of admitting what had happened out under the scorching desert sun in the *Arabian Nights* fantasy she had indulged in so recklessly. So punishingly stupidly…

The Princess took her writhing hands. Stilled them. 'Tell me,' she said. 'Tell me why it was so disastrous for you.'

There was kindness in her voice, and command as

well—but not the command of a princess, but that of a woman, knowing the ways of women. The mistakes they made—mistakes that could ruin lives. Devastate them.

And with a faltering voice, stammering words, Diana told her.

There was silence. Only the sound of birdsong through the open window and the sound, very far off, of a lawn being mowed beyond the rose garden.

'Oh, my poor friend.' The Princess's voice was rich with sympathy, with pity. 'My poor, poor friend.'

The small café was all but deserted. Nikos sat with an untouched beer, his half-brother likewise.

'My father,' said Antoine, 'was not an easy man. He was considerably older than our mother. A difficult, demanding man whom she should never have married. That *no* woman should have married,' he said dryly. 'But there it was—too late. She was his wife. His *comtesse.* And required to behave in a manner he considered appropriate. Which demanded, above all, her producing an heir.'

Antoine's voice was dryer still.

'Myself. And so I duly made my appearance.' His eyes grew shadowed. 'Did my mother love me? Yes— but she was not allowed to spend much time with me. I had nurses, nannies, a governess—eventually a tutor, boarding school. Then university, military academy—the usual drill.'

He shrugged with an appearance of nonchalance.

'In the meantime my mother was lonely. Her life

sterile. When she met your father...' his eyes went to Nikos's now, unflinching '...despite his philandering reputation she believed she had met the love of her life. His betrayal of her—his repudiation of any loyalty to her after their affair had resulted in the disaster that was your conception—broke her. And then...'

His voice hardened, with a harshness in it that Nikos recognised—recognised only too well.

'And then my father broke what was left of her.'

Antoine reached for his drink now, took a long swallow, then spoke again. The harshness was still in his voice.

'He made her choose. Choose what she would do with the remainder of her life. She was entirely free, he told her, to fly to Greece that same day—to throw herself at the feet of the philandering seducer who had amused himself with her. Or, indeed, she was entirely free to raise her bastard child as a single parent on her own, anywhere in the world she wanted. But if she did then consequences would follow.'

He looked at Nikos, with dark, long-lashed eyes.

'She would never set eyes on me again and I would be disinherited of everything but the title. My father could not take that from me when the time came, but everything else would be sold on the day of his death. My entire inheritance—the chateau, the ancestral lands, all the property and wealth of our name. I would be landless, penniless.'

Nikos saw his half-brother's hands clench, as if choking the life-force from an unseen victim.

'She would not do it. Would not leave me to the tender mercies of my father…' His voice twisted. 'To grow up knowing that nothing but an empty title would be his legacy to me. Knowing that she had abandoned me.'

A shadow went across his eyes.

'She felt her responsibility was to me rather than you. That you would be better off raised in a foster home, never knowing her. Thought it would give you some form of stability at least, however imperfect.'

Nikos watched him take another deep draught of his beer, feeling emotion swirl deep within him, turbid and muddied, as if sediment that had long sunk to murky depths was being stirred by currents sweeping in from unknown seas.

Antoine was speaking again, his glass set down.

'When you came to see her all those years ago, as a young man, she knew that nothing had changed and nothing *could* change. Oh, I was an adult then myself, of course, and even my father could not have kept me apart from her, but still he held the threat of disinheriting me over her head. She knew you were financially protected—that your biological father had settled a large amount of money on you, to be given to you when you came of age.'

'He can rot in hell too!' Nikos heard his own voice snarl. 'I never took a penny of that money. He'd disowned me from birth!'

For a moment Antoine held his half-brother's gaze. 'We have not had good fathers, have we?' he said quietly. 'But…'

He held up a hand, and in the gesture Nikos saw a thousand years of aristocracy visible in the catching of light on the signet ring on his brother's finger.

'But I do not think that of our mother.' He was silent a moment, then spoke again. 'Come to her, Nikos.'

It was the first time he'd used his half-brother's name.

'She has a serious heart condition. This operation is risky, and requires great skill from a top surgeon. She deferred the operation deliberately for years, waiting for her husband to die. Only now, with my inheritance assured, can she take the risk.' He took a breath that was audibly ragged. 'The risk that she might die before seeking to make what peace she can with you.'

Antoine gave a long sigh.

'You blame her—I can understand that. I too would be bitter. But I hope with all my heart that perhaps you can at some point bring yourself if not to forgive her, to understand her. To accept the love she has for you despite all she did.'

Nikos closed his eyes. He could not speak. Could not answer. Could only feel, deep in that part of him he never touched any longer, where the sediment of bitterness, of anger, had lain for so long, that there could now be only one answer.

His eyes flashed open. Met those of his half-brother.

'Where is she?' he said.

Diana stood at the wide front entrance to Greymont, with the lofty double doors spread to their maximum extent. Dusk was gathering in the grounds and she could hear rooks cawing in the canopy, an early owl further off, and she caught the subliminal whooshing of a bat.

The warmth of the evening lapped around her, but she could not feel it. Her eyes were watching the slow progress of the two-car cavalcade driving away, down towards the lodge gates.

Princess Fatima was leaving.

But not without leaving behind a gift that was priceless to Diana.

A gift she had immediately, instantly demurred over.

'Highness, I cannot! It is impossible. I cannot accept.'

An imperious raised hand had been her answer. 'To refuse would be to offend,' the Princess had said. But then her other hand had touched the back of Diana's. 'Please...' she'd said, her voice soft.

So, with a gratitude she had been able to express only falteringly, Diana had taken the Princess's gift. And now, as she watched her uninvited but oh-so-kind guest take her leave, the same profound gratitude filled her.

The black cars disappeared down the long avenue and Diana went back indoors. Went into the estate room—her office—sat down at the desk and withdrew her chequebook. With a shaky hand she wrote out the cheque she had longed with all her being to be able to write for so many long, punishing months.

The cheque that would set her free.

Free of the one man in the world she could never be free of.

However much money she repaid him.

Nikos sat in his seat on the jet, curving through the airspace that divided France from England. He stared out over the broken cloudscape beyond the window, his thoughts full. Emotions fuller.

She had been so frail, that woman in the hospital bed. So slender, so petite, it had hardly seemed possible that she had given birth at all—let alone to the two grown sons now standing at the foot of her bed. The son she had chosen over her baby, who had now brought that lost child back to her. And the son who had hated her all his life.

Who could hate her no longer.

Her eyes had filled with tears when they had gone to him. Silent tears that had run down her thin cheeks so that her older son had started forward, only to be held at bay by the veined hand raised to him. Nikos's half-brother had halted, and she had lifted her other hand with difficulty, lifted it entreatingly, towards the son she had abandoned. Rejected.

'I am so sorry.' Her voice had been a husk, a whisper. 'So very, *very* sorry.'

For an endless moment Nikos had stood there. So many years of hating. Despising. Cursing. Then slowly he had walked to the side of her bed, reached down, and for the first time in his life—the first time since his body had become separate from hers at his birth—he'd touched her.

He had taken her hand. For a second it had lain lifeless in his. And then, with a convulsion that had seemed to go through her whole frail body, she had clasped his fingers, clutching at him with a desperation that had spoken to him more clearly than words could ever do.

Carefully, he had lowered himself to the chair at her side, cradled her hand with both of his, pressing it between them. Emotion had moved within him, powerful, inchoate. Impossible to bear.

'Thank you.'

The voice had been weak and the eyes had flickered—dark, long-lashed, sunken in a face where lines of illness had been only too visible—moving between them both.

'Thank you. My sons. My beloved sons.'

She'd broken off, and Nikos had felt a tightening in his throat that had seemed like a garrotte around his neck. Antoine had come forward on jerky legs, sitting himself on the other side of the bed, taking her other hand, raising it to his lips to kiss.

'Maman…'

In his brother's voice Nikos had heard an ocean of love. Had felt, for one unbearable instant, an echo of the word inside himself. An echo that had turned into the word itself. An impossible word…an unbearable word. A word he had never spoken in all his life.

But it had come all the same. The very word his brother had spoken.

Maman.

He heard the word again now, sitting back in

his seat as the plane banked to head north. He felt again the emotion that had come with that word. Felt again the spike of another emotion that had stabbed at him—at his half-brother, too—as their heads had turned at the entry of a man in theatre scrubs.

'Monsieur,' the cardiologist had said, 'I regret, but it is time for you to leave. Madame la Comtesse is required in surgery.'

Fear had struck him—a dark, primitive fear. A blinding, urgent fear.

A fear that had one cry in it.

Too late.

In his head the cry had come—primitive, urgent.

Let it not be too late! Let me not have found my mother only to lose her to death.

And now, as the powerful twin engines of the private jet raced him back across the Channel, he heard that cry again. Felt that fear again.

But this time it was not about his mother.

Let it not be too late. Dear God, let it not be too late.

Not too late to learn the lesson that finding his mother had taught him. The lesson that meant he must now take a risk—the essential, imperative risk that was driving him on. Taking him back to England.

To Diana.

But as he opened his laptop, forcing his mind to a distraction it desperately needed, his eyes fell upon the latest round of emails in his inbox, and he realised with a hollowing of his guts that it was, indeed, too late.

The first email was from his lawyers.

His wife was filing for divorce.

And the money he had spent on Greymont—the money that she owed him—had been repaid. Every last penny of it.

CHAPTER ELEVEN

DIANA STARED AT Gerald across his desk. 'What do you mean, he says no?'

Memory thrust into her head of how she had sat here in this very chair, in this very office, after her father's death, refusing to sell her beloved home. Telling Gerald she would find a husband with deep pockets.

Well, she had done that all right. She'd done it and she'd paid for it.

But not with money. She was abjectly grateful that Princess Fatima had insisted on lending her the money—however long it took her to pay it back over the years ahead.

No, she had paid for what she'd wanted with a currency that was costing her far more. That would never be paid off. Try as she might by breaking the legal bonds that bound her to her husband. They were the least of the bonds that tied her to him. That would always tie her to him…

Her lawyer shifted position and looked at her directly. 'I'm afraid he says he has no wish to agree to a divorce.'

Diana's expression changed to one of consternation—and a whole lot more.

Gerald shook his head. 'I did warn you, Diana,
about this rash marriage. And as for that disgraceful
pre-nup he insisted on—'

She cut across him. 'This has nothing to do with
the pre-nup. I don't want a penny from him. Just the
opposite. That's why I've paid off the sum of every
last invoice he settled, direct to his account. He has
no *reason* not to agree to a divorce.' Her mouth set
in a tight line. 'He has no grounds for refusing me.'

'Except, my dear Diana,' Gerald said in his habit-
ually infuriating manner, 'the law of the land allows
him to do so, irrespective of any grounds you might
imagine you have. And you don't have any, do you?
He hasn't been unfaithful. He hasn't inflicted any
cruelty upon you—'

She blenched. Cruelty? What else had it been,
these past nightmare months since he'd insisted on
having his pound of flesh from her?

Oh, not in a physical sense—her thoughts shrank
away from that; it was forbidden territory and must
always remain so—but in requiring her at his side,
as the perfect society wife. Beautiful, ornamental,
decorative, the envy of all who knew him. The immaculately groomed society wife who could move
in any circles he chose to take her, always saying
just the right thing, in just the right way, wherever
they went.

Outwardly it was a wealthy, gilded life—how
could that possibly be considered cruel?

How could anyone have seen how she bled silently, invisibly, day after day, drained of all hope of release in the frozen chill of his obvious anger with her?

Anger because she'd refused to have the kind of marriage that he'd expected, had assumed they would have—taking it for granted that it would be consummated and then refusing to see why it was impossible… *impossible*!

She dared not think *why* such a marriage as Nikos had wanted was so impossible! She must not let in those memories that made a lie of all her insistence that she did not want a marriage such as Nikos had wanted.

She couldn't afford to let those memories surface. Memories that haunted her…memories that were a torment, an agony of loss…of their bodies entwined beneath the burning stars, bringing each other to ecstasy.

Gerald's dry voice sounded in her ears, making her listen. 'Well, Diana, if you have no grounds for divorce then you will simply have to wait until you can divorce him without his agreement. That will take five years.'

She stared aghast, disbelieving. *'Five years?'*

'Unless you can persuade him to consent to end your marriage.'

He shifted position again, leafed through some papers in a fashion that told Diana he was looking for a way to say what he had to say next.

He glanced across his desk at her. 'You may be able to change his mind, Diana,' he said. 'Your husband has indicated that he will discuss the matter with you personally.'

'I don't want to see him!' The cry came from her. 'I couldn't bear to see him again.'

'Then you will have to be prepared to wait five years for the dissolution of your marriage,' he replied implacably.

She closed her eyes again, emotion tumbling through her. To see him again—it would be torment, absolute torment! But if it was the only way to plead with him to end this nightmarish façade of a marriage—

She looked across at her lawyer. 'Where and when does Nikos want to meet me?' she asked dully.

The uniformed chauffeur who was waiting for her at Charles de Gaulle Airport gave no indication of where he was driving her, but she could see it was not into Paris, but westwards into the lush countryside of Normandy. There was no point asking. Nikos had demanded this meeting and she was in no position to refuse—not if she wanted to be free of the crushing chains of her torturous marriage.

Apprehension filled her, and a clawing dread—knowing she must face him, plead with him for her freedom. She could feel her stomach churning, her breathing heavy, as the car drove onwards.

The journey seemed to last for ever, longer than the flight had, and it was past noon before they arrived at their destination, deep in the heart of the countryside.

She frowned as she got out of the car, taking in

the turreted Norman château in creamy Caen stone, grand and gracious, flanked by poplar trees and ornamental gardens, and the little river glinting in the sunshine, winding past.

It was a beautiful house, like something out of a fairytale, but she was in no frame of mind to appreciate it. Its beauty only mocked the tension in her, her pinching and snapping nerves. Why was she here? Did Nikos own it? Was he renting it? Simply staying here? It could be a hotel for all she knew.

A man was emerging from the chateau, tall and dark-haired, and for a moment, with a tremor of shock, Diana thought it was Nikos. Then the rush to her bloodstream that had come just with thinking she was seeing Nikos again subsided.

'Welcome to the Chateau du Plassis,' he said. 'I am Antoine du Plassis. Please come inside.'

Numbly she followed him, having murmured something in French, she knew not what. Inside, the interior was cool, and there was an antiquity about the place that was immediately was familiar to her. It was a magnificent country house like Greymont—but in another country.

'Is Nikos here?' Her voice broke the silence as she followed her host.

The tall, dark-haired man, who for that heart-catching moment she had thought was Nikos, glanced back at her.

'Of course,' he said.

He threw open a pair of double doors, standing aside to let her enter first. She saw a beautiful salon,

much gilded, and a huge fireplace with the characteristic French chimneypiece. But she took in little
of it. Nikos was getting to his feet from his place on
a silk-upholstered Louis Quinze sofa, and her eyes
went to him with a lurch of her stomach.

He said something in French to her host—something too low, too rapid for Diana to catch—and nor
could she catch Antoine's answer.

Her eyes were only for Nikos, and she was wishing
with all her heart that her pulse had not leapt on seeing him, that her eyes were not drinking him in like
water in a parched desert. He was looking strained,
tense, and she found herself wondering at it.

Then, as her eyes went back to her host, Diana's
eyes widened disbelievingly.

The Frenchman was slightly less tall than Nikos,
less broad in the shoulder, less powerfully made, with
features less distinct, less strongly carved, and there
was more of a natural Gallic elegance in his manner.
His hair was slightly longer than Nikos's, less dark,
as were his eyes, but the resemblance was immediate, unmistakable.

Her gaze went from one to the other.

'I don't understand…' Her voice was faint.

It was Nikos who answered. 'Antoine is my half-
brother,' he said. 'The Comte du Plassis.'

A faint frown formed between Diana's brows as
she tried to make sense of what she did not understand—that Nikos had a half-brother she had not
known existed. It was the Count who spoke next,
his voice with a similar timbre to Nikos's, but his ac-

cent decidedly French, lighter than Nikos's clipped baritone.

'I will leave you to your discussion.'

Antoine gave a little bow of his head and strode from the room. As he closed the double doors behind him the large room suddenly felt very small. A great weariness washed over Diana and she folded herself down in an armchair, overwhelmed by tension, by all the emotions washing through her, swirling up with her being here.

'I don't understand,' she said again.

The three words encompassed more than just the discovery that he had a half-brother. Why had she been summoned here? To what purpose?

She gazed at Nikos. It hurt to see him.

It will always hurt to see him.

That was the truth she could not escape. She could escape their marriage—however long it took her to do so—but it would always hurt to see him. Always hurt to think about him. Always hurt to remember him.

For a moment he was silent, but beneath the mask that was his face a powerful emotion moved. He stood by the fireplace, one hand resting on the mantel, and his gaze targeted Diana.

'I have to talk to you,' he said. He took a ragged breath. 'About things I have never talked about. Because I need you to understand why I have been as I have been towards you these last difficult months. Why I have been so harsh towards you.'

She stared at him, her insides churning. She was

here to beg him to end their marriage, beg him to release her from the misery of it all. She did not need to
hear anything from him other than agreement to that.

'You don't need to explain, Nikos,' she bit out
bleakly. 'It was because I didn't want sex with you.
And since you'd assumed right from the off that, con-
trary to what *I'd* been assuming, sex was going to be
on the menu, my refusal didn't go down well.'

There was a brusqueness in her voice, but she
didn't care.

Dark fire flashed in his eyes—anger flaring. Her
jaw tightened. So he didn't like her spelling it out that
bluntly? Well, tough—because it was true, however
much it might offend him.

But his hand was slashing through the empty air,
repudiating her crude analysis. 'That is *not* why. Or
not as you state it like that! Hear me out.' His expression changed suddenly, all the anger gone. Instead, a
bleakness that echoed her own filled his face. 'Hear
me out, Diana—please.'

His voice was low and his eyes dropped from hers.
His shoulders seemed to hunch, and it struck her that
she had never seen him like that before. Nikos had
always been so sure of himself, so obviously in command of every situation, never at a loss. Self-confident
and self-assured. And in the last unbearable months
of their marriage he'd steeled into his stony, unrelent-
ing determination to keep her at bay, yet chained in-
escapably to his side.

Was the change in him now because she had finally broken free of him?

No, far more had shaken him than the repayment of her debt to him, her demand for a divorce. And as she let her gaze rest on him she felt emotion go through her—one that she had never in all her time with him associated with him.

She tried to think when *she* had ever felt such an emotion before, and what it might be. Then, with a shiver, she realised—and remembered.

It was for my father—when my mother left him.

Pity.

Shock jagged through her as she looked across at Nikos, at the visible strain in his face. Was she feeling *sorry* for him? After all his harshness to her?

She couldn't bear to feel pity! Couldn't bear to see such painful emotion in his eyes. Why was it there? There was no need for it—no cause.

He was speaking again and she made herself listen, fighting down the emotion she did not want to feel for him. She was here to end her misery of a marriage, that was all. Nothing he could say or do would alter that.

'It was because, Diana, your reaction after we came back from the desert showed me that I had never realised just what kind of a person you truly are.'

He paused and she felt his gaze pressing on her, like a weight she could not bear.

'A woman like my mother.'

She stared and saw his gaze leave her, sweep around the room.

She frowned—felt confusion in her mind, cutting through her tortured emotions at his accusation. Why was Nikos here, in the home of a half-brother she hadn't known he possessed?

Her confusion deepened as she remembered how Nikos, when he'd proposed their stark marriage of convenience, had told her that he wanted to marry her for her social background, in order to give him an entrée into her upper-class world of landed estates and stately homes.

But he has that already, here with his brother the Comte. So why—?

His sweeping gaze came back to her. Unreadable. Masked. He moved suddenly, restlessly, breaking eye contact with her. Looking instead somewhere else. Into a place she knew nothing about.

His past.

She heard him start to speak. Slowly. As if the words were being dragged from him by pitiless steel-tipped hooks...

'My mother, Comtesse du Plassis. Wife of Antoine's father.' He paused. His eyes were on her now. 'Who was not *my* father.'

He shifted again restlessly, his hand moving on the mantel, lifting away from it now as if he had no right to rest it there.

'The man who fathered *me*,' he said, and Diana could hear a chill in his vioce that made her quail, 'was a Greek shipping magnate—you would know his name if I told you. He was notorious for his affairs with married women. He liked them married, you see.' Something moved in his eyes, something savage, and her chill increased. 'Because it meant that if there were any unfortunate repercussions there would be a handy husband on the scene to sort them out.' He paused again, then, 'As Antoine's father duly did.'

Restlessly he shifted his stance again, his eyes sliding past her.

'I was farmed out when I was born. Handed over to foster parents. They were not unkind to me, merely... uninterested. I was sent to boarding school, and then university here in France. At twenty-one, after I'd graduated, I was summoned to a lawyer in Paris. He told me of my parentage.'

An edge came into his voice, like a blade.

'He told me that my father would settle a substantial sum on me, providing I signed documents forbidding me from ever seeking him out or claiming his paternity.' The blade in his voice swept like a knife through the air. 'I tore up the cheque and stormed out, wanting nothing from such a man who would disown his own son. Then I drove out here to find my mother—'

He stopped abruptly. Once again his eyes swept the room, but this time Diana could sense in his gaze something that had not been there before. Something that made her feel again what she had felt so unwillingly when he had first started speaking. The shaft of pity.

His face was gaunt, his mouth twisted. 'She sent me away. Saw me to the door. Told me never to come here again—never to contact her again. Then she went back inside. Shutting me out. Not wanting me.

Not wanting the child she had cast aside.' He paused. His voice dropped. 'Rejecting me.'

That something moved again in his eyes, more powerfully now, and it hurt Diana to see it. It was that same look her father had had in his eyes when he'd remembered the wife who had not wanted him, who had rejected him.

'I drove away,' Nikos was saying now, piercing her own memories with his, 'vowing never to contact her again, just as she wished, washing my hands of her just as I had my father, as both of them had washed their hands of *me*. I took a new name for myself— my own and no one else's. Cursing both my parents. I was determined to show them I did not need them, that I could get everything they had on my own, without them.'

There was another emotion in his voice now.

'I've proved myself my father's son,' he ground out, his eyes flaring with bitter anger. 'Everything I touch turns to gold—just as it does for him! And, having made as much money as my father, I gained all the expensive baubles that he possesses, the lavish lifestyle that goes with such wealth—and, yes, the celebrity trophy mistress I had in Nadya! But it wasn't enough. I wanted to get for myself what my mother had denied me in her rejection. My place in the world she came from—the world *you* come from, Diana.'

He paused, his eyes resting on her, dark and unreadable.

'By marrying you I would take my place in that

world—but I would also obtain something else. Something I wanted the very first moment I saw you.'

He shifted his position restlessly, and then his gaze lanced back to her. And in it now was an expression that was not unreadable at all. It blazed from him openly, nakedly. It made her reel with the force of it.

'I could get *you*, Diana. The woman I've desired from my very first glimpse of you. The woman I thought I had finally made my own—the woman I transformed from frozen ice maiden to warm, passionate bride, melting in my arms, burning in her desire for me!'

His voice changed, expression wiped clean. There was harshness in his voice now—a harshness that had become all too familiar in these last hideous months while she had been chained to his side.

'Only to discover that after all we had together in the desert it meant nothing to you. *Nothing!* That to you all I was good for was supplying the money that would save Greymont for you. That only your precious ancestral home was important to you, your privileged way of life. You did not want me disturbing that with my *inconvenient* desire for you.'

She stared at him. The bitterness in his voice was like gall.

He spoke again. 'Just as my mother valued above all else her privileged way of life here at this elegant chateau, undisturbed by the *inconvenient* existence of an unwanted bastard son.'

Diana felt her face pale, wanted to cry out, but

she couldn't. He was speaking again, his words silencing her.

'All these months, Diana, I have blamed you for being like her. For valuing only what she valued. For rejecting me.' He paused. Drew breath. 'It made me angry that you should turn out to be like her. Valuing only the privileged lifestyle you enjoy.' His mouth twisted. 'Nothing else. No one else.'

She could read bitterness in the stark lines of his face, savage and harsh, but there was something else beneath it. Something that seemed to twist her up inside.

He was speaking again, and now there was a tension in his voice, like wire strung too tight, and his strong features were incised with that same tension.

'And *that* is what I need to know! Was I right to be so angry with you? Right to accuse you of being no better than my mother, who only valued all of this?'

His hand swept around the room, condemning in a single gesture all that it represented. His gaze was skewering her, nailing her where she sat. She saw his mouth twist again.

'Are you the same, Diana? Is Greymont all that you are capable of wanting, valuing? Is Greymont and all that goes with it all you care about?'

His eyes were dark—as dark as pits. Pits into which she was falling.

Her voice was shaking as she answered him. Inside her chest her heart had started to pound, like a hammer raining blows upon her. 'You...you knew I married you to protect Greymont, Nikos. You *knew* that—'

A hand slashed through the air. 'But is that all you are, Diana? A woman cut from the same cloth as my mother? Caring only for wealth and worldly status and possessions?'

She reeled. Suddenly, like a spectre, she saw her father, shaking his head sorrowfully, looking at her with such desolation in his face she could not bear to see it. Nor to hear his words.

'I wasn't rich enough for her...your mother—'

She felt her insides hollowing as the echo of her father's words rang in her ears.

She stared at Nikos, eyes distended. There was a spike in her lungs, draining the air from her, and his bitter accusation was stinging her to the quick, the echo of her father's words like thorns in her soul.

Words burst from her as she surged to her feet. His words had been blows, buffeting her. In agitation and self-defence she cried out at him.

'Nikos, I'm sorry—*so* sorry!—that your mother hurt you so much! Because I know how that feels. I know it for *myself.*'

She took a hectic breath, feeling her heart pounding inside her, urgently wanting to defend herself—justify herself. Protect herself from what he'd thrown at her.

'When I was ten my mother walked out on my father. And on me!' Her expression changed, memory thrusting her back into that long-ago time that was searing in her heart as if it had only just happened. 'Like your mother, Nikos, she didn't want me. She only wanted the huge riches of the Australian media mogul she took off with. A man twice her age and with a hundred times my father's wealth!'

She could hear the agitation in her own voice, knew why it was there. She saw that Nikos had stilled.

Her gaze shifted, tearing away from him, shifting around the elegant salon in this beautiful chateau. Shadowing. Taking another breath, she made herself go on. It was too late to stop now.

'She cut all contact. I ceased to exist for her. Was not important to her. So I made her not important to me.'

Her eyes came back to Nikos. He was standing stock-still, his eyes veiled suddenly.

Shock was detonating through him. He had summoned her here to find the truth. The truth he had to discover. The truth on which so much rested. So much more than he had ever dreamt.

Well, now he had the truth he'd sought.

I thought she rejected me because she was like my mother—as I thought my mother to be.

But it was himself. All along it was himself. That was who she was like. Like him she had been abandoned, rejected, as he had felt himself to be, by the one woman who should have cherished her.

A chill swept through him.

She was speaking again.

'My father became my world—he was all I had left. And Greymont—'

A low ache was starting up in her, old and familiar, from long, long ago. Without realisation, her arms slid around herself. As if staunching a wound.

With a dry mouth she forced herself on.

'It was the same for my father. We—Greymont, and myself—became his reason for going on after my mother left him. And it was because…' Her voice changed. 'Because he saw how desperately I loved Greymont—how I clung to it, to him—he vowed to make sure I would never lose it.'

She shut her eyes a moment, her jaw clenching. Then her lids flew open and she looked straight at Nikos. He was stock-still, his face unreadable, his eyes unreadable. It didn't matter. She had to say this now. *Had* to.

'And to ensure that I did he gave up all hope of ever finding anyone else to make him happy. Gave up all thoughts of marrying again. For *my* sake. Because…' She gave a sigh—a long, weary sigh. 'Because he would not risk having a son who would take precedence over me—inherit Greymont, dispossess me of the home I loved so desperately.'

There was a heaviness inside her now, like a crushing weight, as she lifted her eyes to his, made herself hold them, as impossible as it was for her to do so.

'His sacrifice of any chance of happiness for himself made it imperative for me to honour what he'd done. He ensured I'd inherit Greymont—so I had to save it, Nikos, I had to! I *had* to make it the most important thing in the world to me. Saving Greymont. Or I would have betrayed his trust in me. His trust that I would keep Greymont, pass it on to my descendants, preserve it for our family.'

She looked about her again, at the elegant salon with its antiques, its oil paintings on the walls, the vista of the grounds beyond, the sense of place and history all about her—so absolutely familiar to her from Greymont.

Her lips pressed together. She had to make him see, understand...

CHAPTER TWELVE

HER GAZE WENT back to him, with a pleading look on her face.

'It's something those not born to places like this can never really comprehend—but ask your brother, Nikos, whether he would ever want to part with his heritage, to be the Comte du Plassis who loses it, who lives to see strangers living here, knowing it's not his any longer, that's he's had it taken from him?' She shook her head again. 'But places like this demand a price. A price that can be hard to pay.'

She did not see the expression on Nikos's face change, the sudden bleakness in his eyes. He knew just what price had been paid for his brother to inherit. And who had paid it.

There was a hollowing inside him. Yes, he had paid the price, had been farmed out to foster parents. But his mother had paid too. Had stayed locked in an unhappy marriage in order to preserve her son's inheritance. Her husband had been pitiless, refusing to release her, punishing her for not wanting him whilst chaining her to him.

As he, Nikos, had kept Diana chained to his side, punishing her for not wanting him.

Again a chill swept through him.

No! I am not like him!

Denial seared in him. And memory—memory that flamed in his vision.

Diana in my arms, with the desert stars above, her face alight with passion and ecstasy. Diana laughing with me, her face alight with a smile of happiness. Diana asleep in my embrace, my arms folding her to me, her head resting on me, her hair spread like a flag across me.

Each and every memory was telling him what he knew with every fibre of his being, every cell in his body.

She wanted me just as I wanted her. That desire that flamed between us was as real to her as it was to me. So how could she deny it—how?

A 'mistake', she'd called their time in the desert. The word mocked him, whipped him with scorpions.

But she was speaking again, her voice heavy.

'And so I married you, Nikos, to keep Greymont safe. That's why I married you—for that and only that.'

His gaze on her was bleak. 'A man whose touch you could not tolerate? Would not endure? Despite all we were to each other in the desert?'

A cry broke from her—high and unearthly. '*Because* of it! Nikos, are you so blind? Can you not *see*?'

Her arms spasmed around the column of her body, as if she must contain the emotion ravening through it. But it was impossible to contain such emotion, to stop it pouring from her, carrying with it words that burst from her now.

'Nikos—when you came to Greymont and put down in front of me your offer of marriage I wanted to snatch it with both hands! But I hesitated—I hesitated because—'

Her eyes sheared away. She was unable to look at him directly, to tell him to his face. But emotion was tumbling through her, churning her up, and she had to speak—she *had* to! Her arms tightened about herself more fiercely.

'I'd seen the way you looked at me at that dinner. Seen the way you looked at me at *Don Carlo*, and in the taxi back to my hotel. I saw in your eyes what I'd seen in men's eyes all my adult life. And I knew I could not...' Her voice choked again. 'I could not have that in our marriage!'

She did not see his expression change. His face whiten. She plunged on, unable to stop herself.

'But I was desperate to accept your offer and so I persuaded myself that it wasn't there. I believed what I wanted to believe—confirmed, as I thought, by the way you were during our engagement.' She gave a high, hollow laugh, quickly cut short. 'And all the while you were just biding your time. Waiting for the honeymoon to arrive.'

She shut her eyes, not able to bear seeing the world any longer. Not able to bear seeing *him*.

'And arrive it did,' she said, her voice hollow.

Into her head, marching like an invading army that

she had so long sought to keep at bay, came memories. Images. Each and every one as fatal to her as a gunshot.

Her eyes sprang open, as if to banish those memories that were so indelible within her. But instead of memory there was Nikos, there in front of her. So real. So close.

So infinitely far away.

As he must always be.

Nikos—the man who had caused her more pain than she had ever known existed!

'Oh, God, Nikos!' The words rang from her. 'You think me an ice maiden. But I've had to be—I've *had* to be!'

Slowly, very slowly, she made the crippling clenching of her arms around her body slacken, let her hands fall to her sides, limp. She was weary with a lifetime of exhaustion, of holding at bay emotions she must not let herself feel or they would destroy her.

'Being an ice maiden kept me *safe*. Having a celibate marriage to you kept me *safe*.'

There was silence. Only the low ticking of the ormolu clock on the mantel.

'Safe,' she said again, as if saying it could make it so.

But the word only mocked her pitilessly. *Safe?* It had been the most dangerous thing in the world, marrying Nikos—the one, the only man who had set alight that flare of sexual awareness inside her with a single glance. That single, fateful glance that had brought her here, now, to this final parting with him.

Pain seared inside her—the pain she had feared, so much all her life. A wild, anguished look pierced her eyes as she cried out.

'I *needed* to be an ice maiden! I didn't want to feel anything for any man. I had to protect myself! Protect myself from what I saw my father go through! Because what if what happened to my father, happened to *me*? He broke his heart over my mother! Because she never loved him back—'

She broke off, turning away. She had to go—flee! However long Nikos made her wait for her divorce. The divorce that would free her from the chains he held her by.

But he holds me by chains that I can never break! Never!

The anguish came again, that searing pain. A sob tore at her throat and her arms were spasming again, as if she would fall without that iron grip to hold her upright.

And then suddenly there was another clasp upon her. Hands folding over hers. Nikos's strong, tall body right behind her. Slowly, deliberately, he was turning her around to face him.

His hands fell away from her, and she suddenly felt so very cold. She stood, trembling, unable to lift her head to look at him. He spoke. His voice was low, with a resonance in it that had never been there before.

'Diana…' He spoke carefully, as if finding his step along a high, perilous path, 'Your fears have haunted you, possessed you—you must let them go.'

She lifted her head then. Stared at him with a wide, stricken gaze.

'That isn't possible, Nikos,' she answered, her voice faint. 'You, of all people, should know that.' Her expression contorted. 'Those nights we had in the desert… You could not understand why I so regretted them—why I told you it should never have happened. But now you know why I said that to you. Just as I, Nikos…' her voice was etched with sadness '…know why my rejection of you made you so angry. Because it made you think me no better than your mother—the mother who rejected you so cruelly.'

His expression was strange.

'Except that she did not.' He saw the bewilderment in Diana's eyes. 'Antoine came to me—the half-brother I never even knew I had took me to her,' he said. 'He told me the truth about why she had to do what she did.'

Sadly, he told her the bleak, unhappy tale—and then the miracle of his reconciliation with her.

'It was realising how wrong I had been about her, how I had misjudged her, that made me fear I had misjudged *you*, too!' His expression was shadowed. 'And fear even more that I had not.'

His expression changed, his voice becoming sombre now.

'We've both been chained by our past. Trapped. I was trapped in hating the mother who had rejected me, only to find that she had been trapped by her need to protect my brother. And you, Diana, were trapped by the wounds your mother's desertion inflicted on you—trapped by your gratitude to your father, your guilt over his sacrifice for you, your pity for him—the fear you learnt from him. The fear I want so much to free you from.'

'But that fear is *real*, Nikos!' she cried out. 'It's real. It was real from the first moment I set eyes on you, when I knew, for the first time in my life, that here was a man to make me feel the power of that fear. And it was terrifyingly real after our time together in the desert!'

There was a wild, anguished look in her eyes.

'Oh, God, Nikos, that time we had there together only proved to me how *right* I was to be so afraid. You thought I rejected you afterwards because our time in the desert meant so little to me. But it was the very opposite!'

Her voice dropped.

'So I can't be safe from such fear—it's impossible.' She closed her eyes, felt her hands clench before her eyes flew open again. 'I can only try to insulate myself from it, protect myself.'

Even as she spoke she knew the bitter futility of her words. It was far too late. But she plunged on all the same, for there was no other path for her. None except this path now, lined with broken glass, that she must tread for the rest of her life.

'Just give me my divorce, Nikos,' she said wearily. 'It's what I came here to beg for.'

'So you can be free of me?' He paused. 'Safe from me?'

Her eyelids fluttered shut. It was too much to bear.

'Yes,' she whispered. 'Safe from you.'

She could not see his face. Could not see his eyes, fastened upon her. She could only hear him say her name. The words he spoke.

'Diana—what if you could be safe? Not *from* me, but safe *with* me?'

Emotion was welling inside him. An emotion that he scarcely recognised, for he had never felt it in all his life, had never known until he had seen it in his mother's eyes, as she lay so frail, so pitiful, awaiting the operation that might take her from him for ever.

He felt it again now, fresh-made, rising up in him like a tide that had been welling, invisible, unseen and unstoppable, for so, so long.

Since he had held Diana in his arms beneath the burning desert stars.

'Safe *with* me, Diana,' he said again.

That strange, overpowering emotion welled again. It was an emotion full of danger—a danger that the woman he spoke to now, whose clenched hands he was reaching for, knew so well.

Yet it was a danger he must risk. For all his future lay within it. All *her* future.

All our future.

Urgency impelled him, and yet he seemed to be moving with infinite slowness. Infinite care. So much depended on this.

Everything that I hold precious.

That emotion seared him again, rising like a breaking wave out of that running tide within him, so powerful, so unstoppable.

He felt her hands beneath his touch, her pale fingers digging into the sleeves of her jacket. He gently prised them loose, slid them into his hands, drew them away from her body into his own warm, strong clasp.

'Diana…' He said her name again, softly, quietly. Willing her to lift her sunken head, open the eyes closed against him.

'Safe *with* me. *Safe.*'

He took a breath—a deep, filling breath that reached to his core, to his fast-beating heart, and with his next word he risked all—risked the fear that had crippled her for so long, wanting to set her free from it.

'Always.'

Her eyelids were fluttering open…her head was lifting. His hands pressed hers, clasping them, encompassing them. Drawing her towards him, closer and yet closer still.

She came, hesitant, unsure, as if stumbling, as if she could not halt herself, as if she were walking out across a precipice so high she must surely fall, catastrophically, and smash herself on rocks. Her eyes were wide, distended, and in them he saw emotions flare and fuse. *Fear.* And something else. Something she tried to hide. Something that was not fear at all—something that filled him with a rush, an urgency to speak. To say what must now fall from his lips.

The most important, the most vital, the most essential words he would ever say. Words that he had never dreamt in all his life would be his to say. They were filling his whole being, flooding through him, possessing him and transforming him. Fulfilling him.

They could never be unsaid.

They *would* never be unsaid.

'Safe, Diana, in my love for you.'

They were said! The words that had come to him now, burning through all the doubts and fears, all the turbulent emotions that possessed him, burning through like the desert sun burning over the golden dunes.

Love—bright love.

Love that blazed in the heavens.

Blazed in *him*.

Now and for ever.

He folded her to him, releasing her hands, and as his strong arms came around her he felt the sweet softness of her body against his, felt her clutch at him, heard the choking sob in her throat.

He let her weep against him, holding her all the while, smoothing her hair, his cheek against hers, wet with her tears.

'Do you mean it? Oh, Nikos, do you mean it?' Her voice was muffled, her words a cry.

'Yes!'

His answer was instant, his hugging of her fierce. That wondrous emotion was blazing through his whole being now, illuminating the truth. The truth that had started to form out in the desert, under the stars with Diana—so beautiful, so passionate, so precious to him!—whose rejection of him had caused him so much pain.

Pain he had masked in anger. Pain that he no longer had to mask. No longer had to feel. Because now he knew the emotion blazing in him by its true name.

'I love you, Diana. I love you. And with all my heart I hope and pray that you will accept my love. That you do not fear it or flee it! The love,' his heart was in his voice now, heaved up to her, 'I hope that you can share with me, together. '

She pulled away from him, leaning back into the strength of his hands at her spine, her tear-stained face working. At last she was free to say what she had so feared to say—even to herself. What she had kept locked within her, terrified that she had brought about the very fate she had guarded herself against for so long. The tormented and tormenting truth she had admitted to no one—least of all herself—denying it and rejecting it until that fateful day when, with a simple question, it had been prised from her.

One simple question from the Princess—*'What is wrong?'*

And Diana had told her. The truth pouring from her. As she was telling Nikos now, the words choking her.

'I do! Oh, Nikos, I fell in love with you out in the desert. I could not stop myself—could not protect myself. You swept away every defence, every caution. But I knew that I'd condemned myself to heartbreak!' Her eyes were anguished, her voice desolate. 'Because when our marriage ended—as end it must, just as we'd agreed it would—you would move on and then I would become like my father, mourning the loss of a love I should never have let myself feel, but which it was far too late to stop.'

Sudden fear smote her, ravaging her.

'And you *will* move on, Nikos! Whatever you say now, you'll move on. One day you'll be done with me—'

An oath broke from him and all self-control left him. He hauled her back into his arms.

'I will love you *always* Diana.' His voice changed and he cradled her face between his hands. 'I have never known what love is—never experienced it in all my life. Until I found my mother's love for me, learnt the truth about her, about how I had misjudged her. And I feared then that I had misjudged you, too. And I recognised at the very moment you were demanding a divorce what it was I felt for you—what I feared *you* did not feel, *could* not feel, were incapable of feeling.'

She silenced him. With a smothered cry she pressed her mouth to his. Sealing his lips with hers, her love with his. Only drawing back to say, her eyes full, tears still shimmering on her lashes, 'Oh, Nikos, we both bear scars from wounds that nearly parted us, but love has healed them and that is all we need!'

Joy, and a relief so profound it made her weak, was flooding through her. She hugged him close against her, letting her cheek rest on his chest, feeling his strength, his arms fastening around her again. How much she loved him—oh, how much! And she was *safe* to love him—always.

She gave a sigh of absolute contentment. Felt his

lips graze her hair, heard him murmuring soft words of love. Then he was drawing a little apart from her, smiling down at her. She met his gaze, reeling from the love-light blazing in his eyes. She felt her heart turn over, joy searing through her more fiercely yet.

And then the expression in his eyes was changing, and she felt her pulse give a sudden quickening, her breath catching, lips parting, breathless with what she saw in his face. She felt her body flush with heat.

'How fortunate,' he was murmuring, 'my most beautiful beloved, that we are already man and wife. For now I do believe a second wedding night must fast be approaching.'

She gave a laugh of tremulous, sensuous delight, and it was a sound he had not heard for so many long, bitter months. Not since they had found their paradise in the deserts of Arabia—a paradise that now would be in their hearts for ever.

'It's only midday!' she exclaimed, her hands looping around his neck, her fingertips splaying in the feathered softness of his hair. Glorying in the touch of her palms at his nape.

Her eyes were alight with glinting desire. Hunger for him was unleashed within her. And all the memories that she had barred were freshly vivid in her mind, heating her bloodstream. How achingly long it had been since she had held him in her arms!

'Then we shall have an afternoon of love,' he proclaimed, his voice a husk of desire, his gaze devouring her.

There was a cough, discreet, but audible, and a voice spoke from across the room.

'Indeed you shall.' The voice was cool and accented, and very obviously amused.

They turned instantly. Antoine, Comte de Plessis, was standing in the open double doorway, his light gaze resting on them, the slightest smile on his mouth.

'But not, I implore you, until *after* lunch!'

His smile widened, and in his gaze Diana could see fond affection as well as humour.

'I am delighted beyond all things,' the Comte continued, his voice more serious now, 'that the reconciliation which I know my brother longed for has successfully been accomplished.' He bestowed a slight nod upon Nikos, and then Diana, and again that amused smile was flickering at his mouth. 'And I am even more delighted that I may now properly welcome you, *ma chère* Madame Tramontes.'

And now he was walking towards them, as Nikos changed his stance so that Diana was at his side, his arm around her waist and hers around his, drawn close against each other. With Gallic elegance he possessed himself of Diana's free hand, raising it to his lips.

'Enchanté, madame,' he murmured as he lowered it again, released it. 'I can see,' he said, and now his smile was warm, 'that it is quite unnecessary for me to say that you have made my brother the happiest of men. I profoundly hope that it is within his capabilities to make you the happiest of wives.'

His smile deepened.

'And with that concluded…' he raised his hands in another very Gallic gesture and turned to walk back to the doors '…I must, I fear, warn you that your presence in the dining room is required *tout de suite*, for the culinary genius of my chef—upon which he has called in measures previously unsurpassed to present us with a celebratory *dejeuner du midi*—is exceeded, *hélas*, only by the volatility of his temperament. In short, I beg you not to arouse his wrath by a tardy appearance.'

He flung open the doors in a dramatic gesture, infused still with humour.

'Venez,' he invited. 'Love can wait—luncheon cannot!'

Laughingly, their arms still entwined around each other, as their hearts would be entwined all their lives, Nikos and Diana followed him from the room.

From now on, all their days—and all their nights—would be with each other.

For each other.

EPILOGUE

DIANA SAT AT the dressing table in her bedroom at Greymont, putting the finishing touches to her appearance, ensuring she looked her best for her beloved Nikos. And for his brother, and his mother, recovered now from her operation, who'd both arrived this evening to celebrate with herself and Nikos their wedding day on the morrow.

Our real wedding, thought Diana, feeling a wash of love and gratitude go through her. *Which will take place in the little parish church.*

There would be no guests but Antoine and the Comtesse, who would be their witnesses. Witnesses to the union that would not be the empty marriage of convenience that had brought herself and Nikos together, but a marriage of their hearts that would bind them, each to the other, all their lives.

The marriage she longed to make.

She left her bedroom—*their* bedroom, hers and Nikos's—and paused for a moment at the top of the stairs, wondering how she could be so happy. How she could be so blessed. Her beloved home, her beloved Nikos…

But it's the other way round! It's my beloved Nikos and then my beloved home! And it is ours together—and our children's after us.

She descended the marble staircase, glancing in approbation around her. Everything at Greymont was now fully restored as it should be. And now, its beauty renewed, she and Nikos could make plans to open Greymont to the public for periods during the summer. How pleased her father would have been at that!

And at her married happiness. She sent a wish towards him, full of love and gratitude, then smiled at Hudson as he waited benignly at the foot of the stairs.

She walked into the drawing room, her silken skirts swishing. Nikos and his brother rose immediately, and Nikos came to take her hand, walking with her to the woman sitting by the fireside. So petite, so frail, but despite the lines of fatigue around her eyes her gaze on Diana and her son was filled with an emotion Diana knew only too well—for it was in her own eyes too, whenever she gazed at Nikos.

Diana stooped to kiss her, welcoming her to Greymont. It was the first time Nikos's mother had been strong enough to make the journey, and Diana knew that both Nikos and Antoine were treating her like precious porcelain. It was a cherishing kind of care that drew the two brothers ever closer together, and

Diana rejoiced in it. They had so many years to catch up on.

She rejoiced, too, that shortly after her *belle mère* and her brother-in-law had returned to Normandy Greymont would be host again—to royalty this time.

Princess Fatima had wasted no time, on receiving payment in full of the loan she had made to Diana, paid by Nikos, in discovering what had transpired to bring this about—and she was thrilled at what she had discovered. She wanted to see for herself, she informed Diana, and therefore she would honour them with a visit—'to take afternoon tea!' she had exclaimed gaily.

And in the early spring, when the weather would be perfect in the Gulf, the Princess was insisting that Nikos and Diana visit again. *Especially* to take a trip to her brother's love-nest.

'It is where you fell in love with your husband,' she had said, looking sternly at Diana. 'To refuse would be to offend,' she'd warned. But there had been a glint of humour in her eyes as she'd spoken. And there had been a glint of answering humour in Nikos's face as he'd bowed his grateful assent.

'Only a madman would refuse to take the woman he loves more than life itself to the place where the stars themselves blessed their union,' he'd said.

The Princess had sighed in romantic satisfaction.

And taken another scone.

* * * * *

If you enjoyed
TYCOON'S RING OF CONVENIENCE,
you're sure to enjoy these other stories
by Julia James!

THE GREEK'S SECRET SON
CLAIMING HIS SCANDALOUS LOVE-CHILD
CARRYING HIS SCANDALOUS HEIR
A CINDERELLA FOR THE GREEK

Available now!

COMING NEXT MONTH FROM

♦ HARLEQUIN
Presents®

Available August 21, 2018

#3649 THE BILLIONAIRE'S BLACKMAILED MISTRESS

by Lynne Graham

To save her stepmother's job, Elvi agrees to Xan's outrageous terms. He's gorgeous with a damaged side only Elvi sees—but how will he react when he realizes his new mistress is a virgin?

#3650 THE HEIR THE PRINCE SECURES

Secret Heirs of Billionaires

by Jennie Lucas

An exquisite encounter with a Sicilian leaves Tess alone, penniless and pregnant. Until Stefano returns, discovers his unknown heir and reveals he's royalty! Now, to protect his tiny daughter, he'll make Tess his Cinderella bride!

#3651 PRINCESS'S NINE-MONTH SECRET

One Night With Consequences

by Kate Hewitt

For one stolen night, Princess Halina succumbs to notorious Rico's seduction. The consequences land her in royal disgrace. She's hidden away to conceal her secret, until Rico storms the palace! To legitimize his child, he'll make Lina his wife!

#3652 SHEIKH'S PREGNANT CINDERELLA

Bound to the Desert King

by Maya Blake

Requiring a replacement bride, duty-bound Sheikh Zufar commands timid maid Neisha to be his stand-in queen. Their marriage is coolly convenient, but their chemistry burns fiercely... and Neisha's shock pregnancy will test Zufar's iron control!

HPCNM0818RA

#3653 CLAIMING HIS WEDDING NIGHT CONSEQUENCE
Conveniently Wed!
by Abby Green
Nico's marriage to heiress Chiara is purely convenient—until their wedding night! After learning his real reasons for seducing her, Chiara flees. Months later, Nico tracks Chiara down and discovers she's expecting his baby!

#3654 BOUND BY THEIR SCANDALOUS BABY
by Heidi Rice
Tycoon Lukas is shocked to learn he has an orphaned nephew— and infuriated by the electricity sizzling between him and his nephew's guardian, Bronte! When their sensational fire ignites, the dramatic consequences will bind them—forever...

#3655 THE KING'S CAPTIVE VIRGIN
by Natalie Anderson
King Giorgos kidnaps Kassie, demanding information about his missing sister. She knows nothing, but their potent attraction unlocks hidden desires, and they strike a deal. She'll protect his sister's reputation, and Giorgos will introduce Kassie to decadent pleasures...

#3656 A RING TO TAKE HIS REVENGE
The Winners' Circle
by Pippa Roscoe
For revenge, Antonio needs a fake fiancée! He demands shy PA Emma wear his diamond. It's a simple charade, until the passion between them erupts! Now Antonio must decide between vengeance and Emma...

Get 4 FREE REWARDS!

We'll send you 2 FREE Books plus 2 FREE Mystery Gifts.

Harlequin Presents® books feature a sensational and sophisticated world of international romance where sinfully tempting heroes ignite passion.

FREE Value Over **$20**

---

*An exquisite encounter with a Sicilian leaves Tess alone,
penniless and pregnant. Until Stefano returns,
discovers his unknown heir and reveals he's royalty!
Now to protect his tiny daughter, he'll make
Tess his Cinderella bride!*

Read on for a sneak preview of
Jennie Lucas's *next story*
The Heir the Prince Secures,
part of the Secret Heirs of Billionaires miniseries!

He eyed the baby in the stroller, who looked back at him with dark eyes exactly like his own. He said simply, "I need you and Esme with me."

"In London?"

Leaning forward, he whispered, "Everywhere."

She felt the warmth of his breath against her skin, and her heartbeat quickened. For so long, Tess would have done anything to hear Stefano speak those words.

But she'd suffered too much shock and grief today. He couldn't tempt her to forget so easily how badly he'd treated her. She pulled away.

"Why would I come with you?"

Stefano's eyes widened. She saw she'd surprised him.

Giving her a crooked grin, he said, "I can think of a few reasons."

"If you want to spend time with Esme, I will be happy to arrange that. But if you think I'll give up my family and friends and home—" she lifted her chin "—and come with you to Europe as some kind of paid nanny—"

"No. Not my nanny." Stefano's thumb lightly traced her tender lower lip. "I have something else in mind."

Unwilling desire shot down her body, making her nipples taut as tension coiled low in her belly. Her pride was screaming for her to push him away but it was difficult to hear her pride over the rising pleas of her body.

"I—I won't be your mistress, either," she stammered, shivering, searching his gaze.

"No." With a smile that made his dark eyes gleam, Stefano shook his head. "Not my mistress."

"Then…then what?" Tess stammered, feeling foolish for even suggesting a handsome billionaire prince like Stefano would want a regular girl like her as his mistress. Her cheeks were hot. "You don't want me as your nanny, not as your mistress, so—what? You just want me to come to London as someone who watches your baby for free?" Her voice shook. "Some kind of…p-poor relation?"

"No." Taking her in his arms, Stefano said quietly, "Tess. Look at me."

Although she didn't want to obey, she could not resist. She opened her eyes, and the intensity of his glittering eyes scared her.

"I don't want you to be my mistress, Tess. I don't want you to be my nanny." His dark eyes burned through her. "I want you to be my wife."

Don't miss
The Heir The Prince Secures,
available September 2018.

And the first part of Jennie Lucas's
Secret Heirs of Billionaires trilogy,
The Secret the Italian Claims,
available now wherever Harlequin Presents® books
and ebooks are sold.

www.Harlequin.com